AF405295

ASTRID VILLA DORIA

LIFE UNDER FIRE

Life Under Fire
English version — September 2019

ISBN: 978-958-48-7548-8

Writer:
Astrid Villa Doria
villastrid1@gmail.com
Instagram: @villastrid1

Cover page photography
Lidia Corcione Crescini

Translation
Ángeles Sáenz-Chas Prada

Design and Layout
Camila Ahumada Palomino

To my son,
David Duarte Villa,
life of my life,
sea of my hope

CONTENTS

It's around four in the afternoon. It still smells like rain in the city, and the intoxicating aroma of that excellent coffee that is almost ready, awaken all the senses. That same coffee with which I have think about so many times about so many things, the meaning of life, purpose, this and that…, in sum, that pile of ideas that we often call voices that don´t let us sleep. How much we miss that deafening silence, the real one, which invites us to the pure reflection of our being. Life has taught me so many things that it would be selfish for me not to share or to make them known, that's why I decided to write. Many years ago I made a sketch of what tried to be my first book, but after the last storm those writings did not survive, besides I realized that every time a storm happens in your life you have the opportunity to be even better, or to live the rest of your life lamenting for what you lost in it, so I decided the first option, and that's why I decided to share my experiences with those who can take advantage of it, and I deeply hope so.

FALL AFTER FALL, THIS WAY WE LEARN HOW TO WALK

As expected, every human being before walking should know how to get up, and in that we spend all our lives, falling and getting up again and again. It´s precisely that fright of moving forward that encourages us to keep trying. After so much learning we continue with the satisfaction of having done it.

A difficult childhood, an atypical home, lack of affection.

If many people have to live this kind of experience, the difference is, that some decide to become victims and never get ahead, and others decide to be the heroines of their own story. The good thing of this, is that everyone decides who character to be in the movie of his own life.

We are all born capable, some stronger than others in some ways, but the human being is the most perfect being that exists in our world, and the human mind is the most complex machine that hasn´t been able to decipher. There are studies, books, scientific demonstrations, but none comes close to deciphering such perfection, maybe someday we can discover what we are capable to achieve with our minds or maybe we will die in the attempt...

We fell, we were wrong once again and we must, one way or another, go ahead or stay the rest of our lives regretting the pain or suffering that could have caused the fall, depending on how serious it was.

As we grow, maturing, aging, whatever you want to call it, we realize how many times we've made a mistake and how much we've learned from those experiences. The problem is, every moment is unique and one of a kind event. Often we think about the past so we stop living the wonderful present, other times we worry so much about the uncertain future, and the result remains the same.

Sometimes they ask me why I live in one way or another, people are curious to know how other people live, how they face they own life, what their priorities are, and by looking to others, they are missing their wonderful life, their glorious reality.

I live as I think I should live. I can be wrong, right, or fall into a mistake that opens a door for me. Each fall brings its way out, sometimes I fall to get up, in one way or another we put our personal stamp when we walk by life, we see that some people walk with a certain air of superiority, others fearfully, others even dance! There is a little of everything in this world and without those characters, that sometimes leave us speechless, the world wouldn't be the same.

It's nice to get a bit of advice and take those ways of walking in life that feel good for us, with what we feel comfortable, call it beliefs, myths, legends, rules, etc., but the most important thing, is to learn as much as possible from our own experiences considering that each one is incalculably valuable.

We all grow up in different situations with different circumstances, there are endless variables, but hear from other experiences could be priceless, sometimes they can enrich us very much if we know how to take advantage of them.

A COZY LIFE

After so many falls, I felt a comfort moment in my life, and was at that moment when I realized that I was beginning to die. I was like "asleep", I had stopped walking and decided to start the walk again, because that's the point.

Human beings need to be in motion, create business, manage it, move forward, work, study, train, eat, laugh, talk with friends, love relationships, spirituality, are so many things, and sometimes, badly handled, we run out of time, and they leave us with no mood to keep living, but we are much more than that, we are so exceptional beings, that we need all of that and much more, and when everything seems to work, we achieve that comfortable state of mood in that we say: we are happy!

Well... we should be happy without conditioning our happiness to any achievement. Happiness is inside us, not outside, not in another person, animal or thing. Of course we feel satisfaction with our achievements, it is logical, we are emotional being, but how different would it be if we stopped conditioning ourselves and enjoyed every step, every moment, without being paying attention to the neighbor or anyone else.

I had the opportunity to live in an ideal city, a bubble in the middle of nowhere, completely perfect, although the world is much more than that, of c that experience was completely enlightening since I could appreciate the important things.

That perfect city where everyone greets without knowing each other, and after a short while they end up as best friends or worst enemies.

Because of its climatic conditions, this city is like a tropical paradise where everything is perfect. It gave me the opportunity to spend the most important moments of my life, to know my true friends, and to enjoy every inch of the city

Besides the comfort, of enjoy every landscape, every minute, every moment, I also learned how to cook; I'm not ashamed to confess it! I was a spoiled little girl who barely prepared the coffee and burned it in the coffee machine.

But at that point I made the decision to cook and I faced the kitchen like "Rambo". After several burns, stain myself from the hair to the dishware, I learned how to cook, and... Oh! Surprise for more than one, because holding the knife, wearing the apron and a chef hat, all in a perfect match, (because even to learn how to cook you must have style), I faced the cuisine that was, so far, my worst nightmare.

Someone told me with inexhaustible patience, that to learn how to cook, you just had to put love on it, so I did it, well, I also bought books, I downloaded them online, I watched programs, I took notes... to sum up, I put my best in the kitchen. Satisfaction came when at last, I brought, made with my own hands, some delicious food to one of the officers wife´s meetings at the army base in that dreamy city. They all were pleased, and that, for goodness sake, is priceless.

DEATH COMES TO SEE ME, BUT I DON'T PAY ATTENTION TO IT

This is precisely what throws us off balance, that makes us fall and often we don't get up. After a serious illness announcement, most people feel defeated, they can't carry on, it would be better if everything ended, but as always, there are some exceptions, I was it.

I decided to live my own life, and just I can allow people, animals, things, facts, conditions, etc... I decided that cancer didn't fit in my life, it's cancer or me, period, it wasn't up for negotiation; At that time, I don't deny, I thought the same as everybody "Oh, I'm going to die", but in the middle of my perfect city and my perfect life, I said to myself, well, what if I declare the war on it, and I kick it out of my precious body.

I focused on eating healthy, working out, the worse I felt, I got in a better shape, so the truth is, just a few people came to know that I was in that painful process.

I concentrated on smiling, on living, on enjoying every moment, every minute of my life, and I felt that, with the divine help, I'd go on; In fact, I felt it like a revelation, that definitely it wouldn't be difficult for me at all, even though it's a stigmatized disease, and after had those scary stories in my family, both maternal and paternal, where that disease was the main character.

Regular people feels like they want to die and think that their destiny is the same of their relatives, but at that moment I decided to take the lead.

I went to any doctor they recommended me, I think, the best of all was a homeopath. The curious thing about this man, is that every time I went to his medical consulting, he seemed to be younger. That man helped me a lot in this process and, in one way or another, made it bearable, he forbade me from some kind of food, and the truth is, everything was easier.

Of course, if the surgeon hadn't talked me into surgery and removed the tumor from the root, I wouldn't be here to tell.

So much medical treatment was purification for my soul. I became irritable because of medication, I lived alone all this things, because I never told my husband what this treatment really implied, and how he used to work day and night at that time, I hardly ever saw him, so I continued keeping my secret.

For several years I focused in to hide the symptoms of illness, when I got worse I dressed up with all my finery. My hair fell out, I bought hair extensions and wigs, I wore them as naturally as if I had always worn them. They even became fashionable!

I refused to talk about it until someone made me understand that my way of dealing with this disease was a role model, and sharing it could help many women in their tough battle; Actually, nausea and irritability are the most difficult to hide, it's not easy to lose weight, but everything is handled, you just have to want to live, go on, and want to fly high instead of get tired of looking to the sky. You make the decision to live; and although it sounds mean, life goes on, we are the ones who really decide whether to go ahead or fall down on the floor and cover yourself up cowardly. Some people even buried themselves alive. The more fragile, vulnerable and more sorry you feel for yourself, the same way, the illness becomes bigger and neither the best surgeon nor the best drugs will be able to heal you.

OTHER WORLDS DISCOVERY

The alarm rings at about three o'clock in the morning… So run! If you don't want that happens to us like the song says "Nos deja el avión". I have to go to the Bogota's airport after the odyssey of crossing the Colombian Pacific jungle towards civilization.

Three years of jailing didn't finish with the desire to live and take on the world; who said that circumstances could end one's life, definitely declared himself defeated before the battle begin.

Well, I'm going with a suitcase full of hopes and a overloaded baggage, heading to the United States of America, to see if there is such a real American dream or if the Americans are dreaming; Whatever, after several hours of flight I arrived, with my Colombian passport in hand, after the painful initial frisk and passing through immigration, I finally tread foreign lands, and I started to learn how to live in such a different country.

How do we get use to this new different world? I don't know, but for me, that was a new opportunity in my life, even with hair extensions or wigs on my head, but happy to be breathing other airs that don't be purer, far from it, but thanks to all those "gringos" films, to all those canned products, finally, thanks to all of that, I felt so good!

Everything doesn't stop looking like ooooh! But in life nothing's ever perfect, the disappointment begins.

After spending several months sightseeing this beautiful country, I tried to know as much as I can, I enroll in school to learn English language, or "Spanglish", anything, but that helps; Anyways, the "Chibcha" language comes out, strips down, and bored of trying to appear out of the blue in so ambitious country, after so much kick around.

Go up and down on anything that transports you, walking tour, by train, by bus, etc..., after so much hustle and fill the American citizens pockets lashing out of taxes and overload payments, cause I had to divide the luggage by boxes along the trip, since from state to state the load standards change, I arrived at the big apple, according to the "gringos": The World's Capital , because they try to transform the ugliness in beauty, for this reason they are world power and we are a third-world country.

And the patriotic pain begins. I listened to the Colombian national hymn and I burst into tears, well, when you are away all this Colombian things seem nicer and they are more touching than usual.

Every Colombian TV campaign hurt, of course, in Colombia they don't even show them, but here they show the worst, for example the soldier with no legs, the mutilated girl or boy... we seem to be the poorest because they want to see how the old Robin Hood complex works, to see if the rich give to the poor, the paradox is that IT DOESN'T WORK, the poor doesn't become richer neither the rich gets poorer, we have to change our minds to see if one day our beloved Colombia homeland progresses.

LIFE IS BEAUTIFUL, BUT NOT EASY

When everything seems to be perfect it's when is really close to unleashing a hell storm, and after the storm, in sum of the losses that ordinary people usually see, the opportunity to start all over again is the greatest blessing, since we have the chance to rewrite our story as we want it to be.

I remember now the story of Blue Beard. Some women get married while they are still naive about predators, and choose someone who turns out to be destructive to their lives. They have decided to "heal" him with love. Somehow they are "playing house".

You could say that they have spent too much time exclaiming: "Actually his beard is not that blue." Although it could be the woman's partner himself who denigrates her and dismantles her life, it coincides with the innate predator within her own psyche.

As long as the woman is forced to believe that she has no power, and / or is trained to unconsciously don't record what she knows to be true, the feminine impulses and gifts of her psyche will continue to be killed. The predator's deceitful promise is that the woman will become his queen in some way, when in fact he's planning her murder.

There is a way out or a solution to all this, but we should have some kind of key. The key is both permission and approval to know the deepest and darkest secrets of your psyche, in this case, use to be something that negligently denigrates and damages the woman potential.

Raising the appropriate question is the central action of transformation in fairy tales, in analysis and in individuation. The questions are the keys that open wide the secret doors of the psyche.

Yes, I'm not sorry to say, I had a Blue Beard in my life. I got married and I felt like his queen, but after all that romance of unbridled passion vanished, I started to discover who he really was, and don't judge me, because it took me 10 years of marriage to unmask him; It's now a great pride for me, and with my head held high, I stick out my chin and smile on the background of that story. And as the victorious general after having fought his life in a battle, I feel that I wear several honor and courage medals then of having survived that horror story. And it's a paradox for those who know me, they couldn't believe what I went through, because I've always been a woman to be reckoned, a leader in my group, and with effort, I've come out of those cruel situations.

That was both the hardest of all and perhaps the greater learning one.

How was it possible that I came out of a serious illness, I made decisions, I didn't hesitate for a moment, I proceed, I took the treatment, and I faced each of the situations that involved, with height though, the only girl of the oncological center with high heels, makeup, and skinhead. Neither the doctor couldn't believe how proudly I wore my hair extensions and that I didn't care what people might think. When I got to thinking that I was going to die, I called my sister and everyone I could, I gave in bequest all my holdings, everybody was going to receive something from me.

I kept the secret that I was sick until they told me I was going to stay alive. I thought that for no reason I was going to shout from the rooftops about an illness that no matter how much people care about me, they couldn't save me, and in return, I would get all those stories from beyond the grave.

I imagined myself between ladies crying around me, in a dismal gathering with words like:

- "Oh my God, I know a similar story! And what a pity! She died a few months later"

In short, thinking about that was giving me a headache, well the worst was to die, and then there wouldn't be more, then there would be no problem.

I gave the best of me and then, who knew, the same woman strong as steel fell into a deep clinical depression.

That was caused by a husband saying the words every woman dreads:

-"I don't love you anymore."

Wooooooohooo! For God sake!!, what did I do? What was wrong? Didn't he like the dinner?

I was so scared, frightened, I felt like such a small thing, like a bug.

-Oh God! But go ahead, girl!

It was my first reaction after leaving depression;

-Well, I already played alone, and that's not difficult. I got worse...I encouraged myself! I won't come down! I'm leaving the country, I come to my dear friend, partner, and companion and almost sister; Baby, I'm leaving!

I didn't dare to tell all my owns why I made the decision;

Well, we set out to find out the possibilities to fulfill the purpose, it wasn't a long time when that mom intuition, or rather, the "mamasita" sixth sense in my case.

It touched me and in a state of meditation which, at that moment, was very common, I asked myself:

- Why I feel so bad?

I felt worse and worse...

-What happened? I didn't understand.

When I saw a calendar I got curious. After three pregnancy tests, all positive, YES, finally I will be a mom!!

How did it happen?, but we just broke up, so much failed treatments and when I finally made up my mind to don't have a baby, comes to my world that little kid.

I knew since that moment he was going to be a baby boy.

Don't ask me how or why, but I felt it, and strangely enough, in spite of all the pain, suffering and sadness, that little bean growing within me, became that expected miracle, and obviously I felt the world's happiest woman.

I thought it would all settle down, but things were very different, and that's when the cruelest hell began to me.

In a few words, I almost miscarry my baby several times; I had a very complicated pregnancy. After 27 kilos extra and a healthy, beautiful, and so, so cute baby, I realized that life is more than someone emotional attachment, and it may sound very cruel but … I forgot my past and carried on.

AND WHO HAS NOT SUFFERED...

There are situations in life we never imagine can happen to us, however, they happen, and the worst thing is we're usually unready to face them, then we realize of we can be stronger or weaker than we think.

-The situations have to be faced, that's a lie. What if I leave the country? What if I change my name! What if...whatever?

Life will be a bed of roses, and we must remember, to take pleasure with a rose you should know how to deal with the thorns. So I stopped daydreaming and I took the determination to act as a growing up.

I didn't know how, when, or where this "turn around" happened.

The first thing I thought was looking for a good quality of life to David, my son, that sweet little piece of me, my true love.

At that point I imagined that little thing playing and laughing. That was the biggest shot in the arm, the reason what encouraged me.

Well, I'm leaving Bogota, the city of this battle, towards Cartagena.

I should get out of there as soon as possible to keep going, the sad part was taking my son along with me.

No, David is the light of my life, that little one deserves the best cause I waited for him, I dreamed of him for a long time, and he finally arrived, I must do as much as possible to raise him, even with my harmed heart.

When you break a glass, the best thing is to throw it away and buy a new one, but in feelings, it's to take the last piece and assemble it. It's a slow, long, tedious and quite a painful process, but it's possible, no doubt of it, and to illustrate the point...me.

REINVENTED MYSELF

Good morniiiiiiing! It's nine o'clock and I arrive to my friend's house, to organize my work, being a single mom is not easy at all, or as people use to call it, a separated mom (in order not to hurt feelings), since in this modern days there are women who still feel hurt their pride when for some reason they don't make clear enough their civil situation.

What a disaster! That marriage certificate, now broken up, has been a waste of time, endless days for the countdown for divorce, lawyers, and even shoes, because walking from court to office completely wasted them.

Oh God, if someone in good faith had warned me, maybe I'd have listened to him, and I would be saving so much physical and psychological wear. That remind me the past so much that doesn't allow me to get over it, and in my case, divorce was an extremely painful situation.

Well, back to the beginning, that morning of sit around talking and coffee, I decided that was my turn to reinvent myself. Have been an unselfish wife for so many years didn't help at all! Spend the day cooking, cleaning and getting dressed up for a man who didn't care about me!

That's over, and with much honor, I thought my life had to take another direction because I wouldn't live all my life trying to earn money to survive.

How many people haven't spent life trying to make enough money to give themselves the dreamed lifestyle? They end up dying a little bit every day, enslaved either to a desk or to the daily tasks. Well, I'll take time for everything, if I was a 10, I'll become a 20, but that´s just for me, not for anybody else.

At that time my "image designer" and I went shopping, I needed to change everything, the image counts, and in this world where is all about the presentation, much more; I realized that university degrees aren't painted in any visible part, and we are talking about a woman who has more degrees than a thermometer, (as the manager of a prestigious hospital told me when I brought her my cv).

It's true, you have to be and look like a smart person, because nowadays the image worth it, and it also costs, if it wouldn't multinationals wouldn't invest millions in products marketing and advertising, and without going too far, we must represent ourselves as best as possible, the main rule is: you must look stunning or don't go out! You never know who you will find around the corner, that applies for the future father of your children,(the ones you already have and the ones you'll have), your ex-husband's new wife, that special friend's mother, that school or university's classmate, etc... You never know.

Anyway, I reinvented myself and it works like a charm. In those moments I understood that a woman doesn't spend, she actually capitalizes herself.

THE GLORIOUS JOB
OF BEING A MOM

As they told me so many times that I couldn't be, the truth is, my son is a true miracle, he's my blessing but sometimes, as all the babies, he's a little bit dramatic, spoiled, and he had got his father's temperament, they say the temperament is inherited but the money is not, now I understand the saying "like father, like son".

My one year and a half great miracle is a world of emotions for me, every day comes out with something new, and that comes out expensive, of course, I understand now a friend of mine who told her husband when he insinuated her to have another baby, "Oh Love, when you have Julio Iglesias's wealth to pay baby's food...as many babies as you want!"

Well, thanks God, or to whoever you believe, for your children lives, because are those small walking tornados who encourage us to get up every morning to be a better person. It can be the world's lower-pay work, but as a credit card advertising says, "There are things money can't buy".

They can be whatever they are, for example, having broken anything expensive newly bought, but through a tender look, a satisfaction smile or with a simple "dadada" they fix everything!

The world keeps spinning and if we stop thinking about a minute, the truth is we're left behind, and it isn't the world's fault, it's our fault because we aren't being strong enough or fast enough to keep going and catch the beat to leave a life mark, the truth is, I don't know anybody who has returned from afterlife, so let's enjoy what we have and face what we can.

If the most difficult thing is to lodge them as guests for nine months, well, 8 months in my case...thank God for that, who knows if I could stand one more day; my son was great, it'd be so much fruit salad with ice cream, so much oatmeal or so much shrimp and more shrimp which I ate in pregnancy, but that baby was huge!

Now I remember it happily because it happened, I passed through it oh goodness, but my pregnancy was horrible, the hormones to the max, dizziness, cravings, mood swings, the frightening love for the father of my son, my ex-husband today who made my life impossible. Is precisely at that moment when they give me the best news they've ever given to me. We were legally separating, and I had thought the tumor was the worst of my life, no, the separation hurt me much more.

I loved him, do I call it love?, rather affection, well, whatever, he hated me the same way back, because in one way or another, my situation was interfering his bachelor life, he had more than chick and he was writing the same poems for all of them .

Oh surprise!! The day I realized that he was sending the same ones that I wrote for him.

I stopped knowing about him long ago, I stopped caring about his life, but at that time, when I was pregnant, I became the best detective in the world. On second thought, the twenty-seven kilos over probably had something to do, I couldn't even walk, the last month I was in a wheelchair, my spine collapsed.

Anyway, I recovered and after the C-section and my baby out, I focused in take care of myself and try to recover my weight.

It wasn't easy, it took me a year and several months, but I still keep trying to recover my fit, at least, I'm healthy.

As a first time mom, I did it wrong more than once, I didn't know how to carry the baby, I didn't know how to breastfeed him and then I refused to believe gravity took effect.

ILLUSION OF LOVE

Nothing more beautiful than a love illusion, I am sitting over a coffee in the bookshop that love, in the city historical center, that glorious place where I'm going to meet my friends, partners and brothers, where I go to have a coffee, to read or just to clarify ideas and be entertained with my things. Come to me, that feeling of love, I have no idea of what happened, I don't know if it was the background music, my favorite, jazz... blues... that kind of style! I don't know, but I felt alluded to, at that moment I felt that I really was in love, but of life itself. At that moment I couldn't stand it and took out a pencil and a sheet and I started, as a little girl making the letter to Santa, to write a long list. But this time it wasn't a wish list, It was a appreciation list. That list was about thank to all that I had achieved so far with much effort, with much sacrifice, but I got it, and with tears in my eyes I wrote and wrote, until I was late to go to the gym. To sum the thing, I said thank you even for the underwear I was wearing because it was new! And that was when I got separated and decided to return to Cartagena, when I made the decision that I would start from scratch and that's how it was!

I know that it isn't easy to think that, at that point, when you are already at that stage in your life where you have achieved most of the necessary material things to lead a decent life, you must say: to hell with it!! I don't give a shit!!

There is no love purer than one self's; When we learn to love ourselves we can share that love with others, and there isn't greater love than our eternal father's, even if we make mistakes so many times, He is always there for us, ready to give us a hand or carry us in his arms. Well, at this moment of my life, to start all over, I was enveloped in that pure love who is God, the Father, and I know that thanks to Him I have come alive. He is the master, as they say, the best thing that has happened to me in life is life itself.

I live in love with life, and I realized that free things are precisely the ones that worth more, like that pleasant awakening and seeing the sun, and when I say pleasant it's because if we're alive and healthy, there's nothing more pleasant than that. Poor the one who hasn't learned to enjoy what he has and keeps complaining about what he doesn't have yet, and probably never will, because life gives you insofar as you know how to handle situations. That about walk around complaining about everything and blaming everyone is pointless.

God's love is endless and can reach us, as much as we are willing to receive it.

DOUBLE BETRAYAL

"Mascarada", an old TV soup that by my young age at that time they didn't let me see, is the name that I want to bring up, when the internal conflict between good and evil begins. To have gone to hell and come back is not easy at all, but it seems that one spark or another went through the great beyond, because when you have a pure soul, you trust, and that was precisely what happened to me, I trusted in a so-called friend and… oh, surprise! I hear that she is my ex-husband's new wife; How can be possible? I almost died for the umpteenth time that day I found out.

Everything I confessed to her, everything I told her, obviously, she was my friend and who better than a friend who went through a separation process to share my things, I thought she understood me, that she listened to me, that she loved me as much as I did, but painfully I can tell that it wasn't like that; how wrong I was, how silly I was, how naive; The fact that one has values and integrity doesn't mean that the rest of the world have them, I learned it with tears the day I found out that this pair had a fairly long relationship, among other things, what a Machiavellian plan of this two; From my ex, I expected that about him, and it doesn't surprise me, that's truth, but from her, poor thing …! There are so much women in this world, but NO, he had to get involved with one that I appreciated, so much, I even defended her when some time ago he forbade me her friendship, since as I said before, she had separated in not very good terms of my husband's best friend.

NEW HISTORIES TO LIVE

Life itself is like a book, you can write what is born from your heart in it; sometimes you have to close chapters, finish books and even close libraries!

This happens when you live so long with a person that after more than ten years…wasn't your man! It even sounds funny, and "the sorrow of many is a fool's consolation", but I won't be the only one, thanks God it just was a decade and not two or three. Life is now! In time, everything happened, who knows what would have happened to me, because at least today, with youth, divine treasure, I was able to recover part of my figure before pregnancy, and every time I look in the mirror and see my abs with a C-section in the middle, I say: "It was worth it"

I could afford to be painted naked! Without any kind of shame or inhibition, I felt very comfortable, all that sweat in the gym has its reward, besides of having lost part of the twenty-seven kilos I gained in pregnancy helped me to recover part of my figure, although that's not the most important thing, I feel healthy, in good shape, no more walk three blocks and feel drowned, although I walk in heels under the burning sun , juggling, stepping with style every day, because most of us take great pains to give a pleasant image to the rest of the world; By respect for humankind we comb our hair every day, we have perfect nails, we go fragrant and make-up even if it takes a few more minutes of the daily hurry, but that touch-up must be done.

You have to project the best image!

It's like going to a restaurant; the dish may have an exquisite taste, but if it doesn't look nice, who will even taste it? Well, not me, thank you! And I'm sure that most of us do not either. Of course, there are exceptions, and God bless women because they are beautiful and glamorous, as I consider, being a woman is a sign of beauty and glamour already.

So I decided to live my new life, and I live it day by day, it's beautiful to know that each day brings its own challenges, and sometimes in a single day so many things and so many emotions can come about at the time, that you end confused and even tired, and that was precisely what happened to me recently.

It was that ten o'clock in the morning and I was heading at a hasty pace, (I live literally running, because of my work, which I love) to the old parking to cancel my rental agreement cause it was several blocks away from my office, so I looked for a closer one. I proposed to pay and tell the manager that I wouldn't park anymore there, when, suddenly, he gives me a book, signed by its author, a poetry book. The manager told me that this author autographed one of his many copies for me.

Thanks!, what could I do?, was during the Valentine's month, when I spent the day with a girl (member of our society) talking until sunrise on the balcony of her house. I accepted, and less than two hours since then, at work I keep thinking about the mysterious man.

The only thing I know about him is that he parks his car in the same place I used to park mine, how did he know that my hobby is reading?

How did he know that I love poetry? Or maybe he didn't know and was just a coincidence. But I'm a romantic, so I made a film, and I enjoyed it!

Then I went to one of the offices that I visited in my commercial work when the assistant told me with a slightly telltale smile: Look what somebody left to you. I couldn't believe that the beautiful thirty yellow rose's bouquet was for me; what is happening? It couldn't be the same person, obviously not, but the assistant who gave me the roses didn't tell me who the one who had such a beautiful detail was!? How did this other person know that I love having fresh flowers at home?

Well, almost all women love flowers with the exception of those that associate them with funerals, they aren't lack

In short, as they say, "The universe conspires", but this is a little suspicious...what kind of signal is that?

Come on, let's see the bright side; I was a bit disappointed during those days because walking alone isn't easy and I try to keep busy.

IN A WAITING MOOD

When I expect an important result I can't feel good, I freak out, is just a sign of how human I am, the most terrifying thing for me, I don't feel sorry to tell you, it's to go back to the breast cancer exam, I feel scare, and it would be another story if I hadn't gone through that painful experience, and if I had a couple, but as neither one nor the other, head up high and feet on the ground, keep myself together and calm down. I wobbles before the possibility of bad news, the important thing is to find it out on time and there's no a small battle, life isn't for cowards, nor weak, the same nature in its wonderful process of selection is in charge of doing the work, so at this time of the game I'll decide to be brave and face life once again.

It does frighten me, of course, I'm not made of ice, I am human and quite sensible; if you know someone who even cries with the TV advertisements you'll know what I mean, weeping from birth and so proud of it. What a delight when you get that pain out your chest, or at least part of it, feels a lighter weight, renewed, there isn't better therapy, and that crying is not only for women. I'd like to see a man with eight months of pregnancy, dead tired, to see who the weak sex is.

I know women who have more guts than the best war strategist and I know men who are so sensitive that I've seen them cry and have appreciations of life that years ago would not fit in the masculine or "macho" vocabulary. But is this human condition what makes us sensitive, beings full of emotions that are, coincidentally, those that make us feel alive.

Those emotions...That emotion of paying the last fee of a debt from years ago; that emotion when he finally answer that YES, that emotion in front of a positive pregnancy test, (doesn't apply to unexpected pregnancies), the emotion in your degree, the emotion of driving your first car, that car you just bought, all those emotions we can feel along our life, those that really make life worth.

TO FACE THE PROBLEMS YOU HAVE TO TURN THEM INTO SITUATIONS

The best thing with problems is that they make you grow as a person, there will always be all kinds of situations in life, and the best way to deal with them is to level up; A very simple example is the economical situation.

People still ask themselves why are there economic abysses between communities, why there is so much money in the world and at the same time so much poverty. The power of the mind is what makes the difference, if you have ten dollars in your pocket and you owe one; it's not a big deal for you. But if you have fifty dollars and you owe a hundred... then you are in trouble. There's a difference, it's at this moment when you ask: what should I do to turn that problem into a simple situation, as it happens in all other life aspects?, and it's just the way you handle different situations which helps you overcome the inconveniences. A problem can't be solved with the same mind that has created it, you have to change your mind, your ideas, your point of view.

What you've been doing is not working so something must be wrong.

Everyone, each of us has all kind of situations to face: economic, psychological, social and even spiritual, there's everything in the Lord's vineyard, and no one imagine that this can happen, until it happens.

I've been to thousands of meetings where tragedies are the favorite conversation's topic. I still don't understand while there are so many good things in this world, people love to waste their time talking about the negative, and the worst thing is they unconsciously attract it to their life.

I decided to get away as much as possible from this type of people, who didn't help, they only gave me stomachache generated by situations that I should solve but I can't; very similar case happens with television and those programs that, in one way or another, influence your daily behavior, unconsciously there are things that are left engraved of dramatic situations in a soap opera, or even worse, the stress generated by a real situation.

Beware of the negative emotions that can trigger serious diseases, it's curious, but science has advanced so much that today the stress is the disease of the century and is the trigger for other diseases, so, take care of yourself, prevent Stormy relationships, stressful situations and all that negative part in the environment, we must do our best try for ourselves.

LOVE OR COMFORT?

In a conversation with a great friend the matter came up.

- How are you doing?

- Very well and improving.

I answer with a confident and warm tone.

- I just finished with my girl.

- How did it happen?

- Well, you see, women are complicated!

- Women must be loved, not understood.

- What would you look for in a man?

- Company, affection, moments to share, to feel loved, valued, respected, someone to laugh with, to tell you little or much of the day by day, moral support and a point of view different from mine to evaluate situations, somebody who complements me and make me feel special.

- Well, that's very different from what many women expect from their partner. I realized that most of them are looking for support, but not that kind of support, but an economic kind.

- It's complicated, we are in Colombia where nothing is easy and there are people with a sexist thoughts, where the woman thinks that it's the man who must provide the money for the family, it's something repetitive, in most homes this is what you see, the mother stays at home raising the children and the father goes to work to provide them.

- Yes, but the last girls I've met think that because they're dating them, they already have the right to be maintain. I'm a generous man and I don't see anything wrong with supporting your partner economically, but after a while it becomes to be a burden or an obligation, that's when the situation becomes uncomfortable.

- Not all women are the same, just as not all men are the same.

- I think I didn't meet the other kind of women, those who believe it's an obligation to pay the rent, services, the university, clothing and all the expenses of the family. I met some girls that want to take advantage of the situation.

- So you have to evaluate who you are getting with into a relationship before generalize, those experiences aren't the excuse to judge the rest of women, there are exceptional beings, capable of maintaining a home completely by herself, and also they have the energy to be moms, hard workers and women in every meaning, you should pay a little more attention to detail and be able to evaluate that person whom you plan to share your time.

It isn't easy to find a person whom shares emotions with and experiences, who make you get butterflies in your stomach or even the entire zoo.

Is a variety of situations that confabulate to make things work between two people. I think it's not as easy as it seems to be.

When you see a person in the street and it attracts you physically it's the first step, then the knowledge phase that sometimes is complicated, starting with the adaptation to your couple's day routine.

MATURITY

Now I am thirty-something years old and the maturity it gives to you, not the age, but suffering, after checking firsthand that the pain goes away, and hope returns intact!

If at this point of my life I managed to survive to a divorce with all its consequences, any other love punishment wouldn't kill me.

I had become a veteran of love's wars, marked with a wound of heartbreak. I'm no longer a girl looking for the man of her dreams; I became a woman looking for someone who is capable to make her dreams come true.

Only God knows if that man actually exists, or is only the product of a mind tormented by loneliness; At this point we end up forgiving everything, but not accepting it, which is the big difference. It's like when they ask us about a controversial topic and the typical answer is: I respect your opinion, but I don't share your point of view!

In the course of the days, in our daily life, when we settle in a period of time and we are in a comfort zone, if we are clever, we can realize before we die trying to earn a living, either in an office or in other job whatsoever.

One day I started to get into the task of analyzing my own life, I always got into analyzing my friend's, because at the end of the day she is the one who tells me everything every day, so we act as psychologists with a doctorate degree, even in couple issues.

If we start to analyze, nobody has the absolute truth in any subject and it should be forbidden to walk around giving advices, knowing that in the first place we must analyze ourselves.

And there was I, with a blank notebook, ready to do the most complete analysis of my life, to see if I had learned something or not, knowing that life is such a good teacher, and if you don't learn the lesson, it repeats it to you.

IT HAPPENS IN MOVIES
IT HAPENS IN REAL LIFE...

Time passes by and you don't realize until you go to your closest friend house and you see your goddaughter who is already a woman, and a beauty...with those geisha eyes, that are able to immobilize any man, "Madrinaaaaaaa!!", she hug me, I remember the time she wasn't reach my waist and today is almost of my height, for God sake!, I feel so old; but the sun's old and still shines and that's why I go to the gym, I eat as healthy as I can when I'm not in the company of my friend who is able to sabotage any diet, with the most infallible ablative anesthesia (the oldest one), and in those amazing talks we almost fixed the world. Who can resist the temptation of a good fast food? But hey... that's life, a constant going forward and better don't look back, if the past wants to come back and talk to you, don't listen to it, believe me, he has nothing new to tell you.

The thoughts seeing my doll, of a scandalous beauty raised to the highest level, left me the sweet taste of the lived things. Nobody can take that away from me. And if I had to live it again, it wouldn't take away anything because without suffer there isn't a real comparison of what is good and what it isn't, what is worthwhile are those joys that, although temporary, are great. And that's what life really is made of; it's full of small things!

And every little thing is a link, a constant cycle, a push and a pull of experiences that, either if they are for yourself or to share them, they form a perfect gear called life and you have to live it regardless of your age. Each age brings its own magic, its charm to learn and discover, and if along the way you lose, then losing by learning, it's not losing.

I am proud of these moments of my life. I feel complete thanks to God; I try to balance as much as possible most important things in my life, every day I feel a progress, I grow as a person, and I help those around me to grow as well, because this work doesn't end till the day I'll die.

To get up with a good coffee and a good book for adults (because the erotic thematic), makes me feel that I have been growing up and I am comfortable with my sexuality, since at this point of the century and despite the so criticized machismo, many women aren't resolve to read one of these readings that more than enriching, fascinating and exciting, make us know ourselves.

You just have to follow what you really feel, what you really want and desire; Of course, be careful, because after those long hunger periods it's probable that any cheap food taste as a lobster.

LIFE READINGS

Desiderata: "Read, read and read until you find your favorite book."

As I may concern, books are the food for the soul, knowledge and life experiences are the only thing that belongs to us, the rest is borrowed, either by time or by life itself;

If at some point we were handed a manual to learn how to live and to get over day by day situations, maybe it would be too boring.

It would be something like...

Manual for a better life:

1. Get up early in the morning because "The early bird gets the prime time". And with the right foot.

    The truth, I don't imagine myself in the morning, around dawn, trying to find my glasses by touch and, as if the effort was not annoying enough, try to coordinate which is the right foot to get out of bed.

2. Keep calm in difficult and stressful situations. We know that controlling emotions is a sad thing and in the end you end up getting sick; There is nothing more delightful than shouting and raising your voice when you feel the need, leaded by the emotions, laughing out loud till the neighbor get mad... who cares what the neighbors think? Is not their business, unless they pay your rent or your bills.

3. It's so easy to criticize situations from the viewer perspective, but once inside the whole situation, it is very difficult to be impartial and control yourself. I have met those types of people who don't get upset in practically any situation, the same ones that I have seen ill until dyeing because of heart problems; the emotions must be felt, lived and handled, not necessarily annulled or controlled, which is completely different.

4. Don't get attached to anything or anyone. It sounds so nice, but whoever has no dependency cast the first stone. I'd like to have a dependency detector to avoid falling into them.

5. Enjoy every moment of life as if it were the last. Yes of course, that exercise lasts a while, until we realize we are again immersing in the daily routine, we forget and return to the cycle. A classic example is that usually few people from Cartagena enjoy the sea; usually most people who were born by the sea forget that they live in an earthly paradise. Well, that depends on tastes, but when we take things for guaranteed, we forget that they exist. Who didn't buy a blouse and in the first weeks you wear it again and again and it feels like it's the most wonderful blouse in the blouses' universe and few days later it ends in the deepest darkness of the closet; or the car that we so much dream of when we finally have it, the emotion and rush lasts only for the first few months. It happens even in relationships.

6. Guard your body which is the soul's temple. It takes too much willpower and conscience to put this theory into practice, it's not easy to get up from Monday to Friday at 4:30 a.m. to go to the gym, and then run to get ready to go to work, going up and down all day long and then prepare yourself to enjoy the most beautiful we have, the family members at home.

I wish there was a life manual, but it's more interesting to create your own through your own experiences. There are books, documentary films, lectures, talks, and even courses, but I think that what really works is what comes from the heart, what we do with love is what gives us the best satisfaction and ends up working in the best way.

As for the body care, extremes are dangerous; the secret is to try to keep a balance to be in a good shape.

Nobody has the absolute truth in anything and therefore doesn't give us the right to want to handle somebody else's life, with our own is more than enough. If one day people would be interested in their own business, instead of blaming external situations, the past or the people around them, and they would began to make a better world, an idyllic world... and false.

OF LOVE AND FRIENDSHIP

We are naturally social beings, therefore we are surrounded by people, now we have to analyze: what kind of people?, based on the fact that we are not perfect, when we surround ourselves with friends, people that we really end up loving, that friend who looks like an older sister or the one who looks like the youngest, the other one that looks like a mom, a scold one, and the mollycoddling one, friends who look like uncles, dads, siblings, etc. I personally think that friendship, as long as it's honest and healthy, should be for a lifetime.

There is no better psychologist than a friend who has lived the situation by your side, they end up being and feeling part of the situation, but seeing the raw reality is good to picking up the reins again, to continue with more encouragement or simply to change the perspective and the situation management.

I completely agree of we can't make it alone, and there are times that we must be more rational and despite of our developing country culture, believe in a professional capable of listening to us and giving us the most accurate perspective of the situation. The false thought of "I heal myself", "I cope on my own", yes, we all fall at some point of our lives in that macabre mental game which the only thing that achieves is to step back into important factors, because we believe we're the super powerful..., so we end up exhausted, sometimes even anxious and with worse problems than we had before. You have to brought down your pride and rely on a friend, partner, family member of more confidence, psychologist or mental health professional.

Of course, don't overwhelm the people who appreciate us with such a thing, one issue at a time, when one is solved the other will arrive, always respecting the spaces, personalities and points of view that may not been even close to ours.

SOUL RICHNESS

Experiences must be treasured and shared as much as possible, cause returning to life part of what it gives us every day is the healthiest thing we can do; Every day we face situations and each being approaches and treats them in a very individual way, that is precisely the good thing of not being all similar, each one reacts differently, each one faces their fears, insecurities or shortcomings in a very different way and also puts their personal stamp.

In the same way there is no need to learn from other people experiences and to approach situations from various perspectives to be able to face them as we think.

It's nice to feel rich and valuable inwardly, that feeling of having nothing but having everything.

When I left the city of Bogotá with my newborn baby in my arms, I had lost everything but I was carrying even more than that I lost, we always recover the material things faster than we imagined, what is really worth it is what we can neither measure or buy; My suitcase instead of clothes, shoes and toiletries, which is what people usually carry on a trip without return, was overloaded with love, hope, pride of being finally a mother, many expectations in a better future, nobility, humility , anxieties and desires of overcoming. All of this, and my heart's joy because I was going to start the closing of my life's chapter, to start a better one.

Likewise, as Rome wasn't built in a single day, I didn't get ahead immediately or magically, things are being solve, one issue at a time, with a slow but firmly and above all very secure pace. At this time I still have issues left , but that's what life is all about, learning every day the best possible way to get ahead, to overcome events and get the most out of all those experiences.

LEGALLY FREE

Time passes by in a particular way, besides to getting older physiologically we grow in experiences and we are treasure special situations and experiences, sometimes we don't even realize how everything happens, we just wait and that stay becomes eternal, like a few minutes, but underwater.

When we're given dates to meet, we see them far or near depending on the situation that accompanies them, the secret is not to give up and focus on something else. If we would be integral beings, this shouldn't be impossible.

Well, many times I prayed God that my uncertain situation ended on the best terms, and that's the way it was; Although it's this subject of my life that has hurt me the most and it's been difficult to face so far, everything has a way and sooner or later it takes it.

Seeing my ex with different eyes, helped me a lot, I see him now from another perspective, he's the father of my son, it's that being with whom I must maintain the best communication and that is when I remember how we were the perfect couple. We were married for years but actually it was a long courtship, and we must give him the credits, he was the man I loved for so long and he knew how to keep me by his side, even though things don't work anymore, now and onwards I only wish him the best. Every day I pray that God bless him with a good woman, with a good fortune and a good discernment so that he knows how to face each of the situations that lie ahead and we will have to share, thanks to that wonderful child, our son. The same one that with his jokes makes us laugh together again. That son that with his tenderness makes us speak calmly and relaxed again.

That son who reminds us that one day we loved each other with the soul, and from the heart, is the one who encourages us to have the best relation in the middle of an assertive communication that I hope, soon will be more fluid for the good of all.

It was time for that especial signature and after a very good talk among all the officials, with bells and whistles, with much sadness, nostalgia and melancholy, we both agreed not to continue the papers war and sign the peace agreement, because that fruit of so much love deserves it.

What does it feel like? It was the particular question asked by several people that day; what I felt, probably no one else has felt it through this situation... or maybe vice versa, almost everyone who is involved in these issues has felt it.

I felt several things; the first: Like if you must lose an essential part of your body, since that depends on your life; nobody would like to have a limb amputated, but if your life depends on it, with the pain of my heart, you must.

I also felt like when you carry a huge, very heavy suitcase, but after a while the body gets used to it and believes that it's part of the normal weight, therefore, when the suitcase is released, it's when we realize that it didn't belong to us.

Then came the phantom pain, the same one that patients suffer when they amputate them a leg or an arm and they continue feeling it, it's not easy to get used to it, but in the end it's healthy to accept reality.

There will always be situations, there will always be memories, but as time goes by, all situations will gradually be over.

MENTAL BLOCKS

After painful events happen, the mind tries to protect itself from this type of situation and what it does is to block everything that has to do with it; it's like when we use the internet search and we write a word to look for related topics, and then they come out like fifteen pages all with the underlined word or with the meanings very close to what we are looking for; likewise, the brain stores information and also specializes in alerts to prevent us from harming ourselves in any way.

As it happens after unfortunate events series, the smallest show of affection begins to hurt, wherever it comes from, it doesn't matter, that doesn't mean that the heart becomes a stone, not at all, it just means that we are human beings, that we feel, and if we have a wound we simply need to heal that wound before uncovering that lacerated part again.

It's not easy to face so deep suffering degrees, so delicate, where the brain uses certain alarms of alert and care for, it gets to a blockage so intense that even a simple friendly word of affection which is full of love hurts and seeks take distance to avoid getting involved and to experience again a degree of suffering, although had been less.

A very smart person intuits it, draws its conclusion and tries to handle the situation expecting positive results; someone less smart just criticizes; someone even with a lower intellectual level just doesn't care, since he will not understand this type of situation in a million years.

There are several ways to deal with and treat these blockages, but the best remedy is time, and that's when conscious decisions for continuous improvement are made.

When a snake bites you, the only way to avoid further damage is to take the poison out, just as there are things in your life that are poisonous, you must take them out as soon as possible, and at that time you reflect and draw conclusions, which serve to grow; Seeing other's faults doesn't make you better than anyone, the important thing is to stay away from the negative and see inside to get the best out of you.

EVERYTHING HAS ITS END, NOTHING LASTS FOREVER

ALICE: How much time is forever?

RABBIT: Sometimes forever is just a minute.

That is one of the famous sentences of the well-known book "Alice in Wonderland," and she is as right as my grandmother when she said: "Baby, don't get married so in love that you idealize your partner." The secret is not to lose the reality perception.

Oh God! Wise words! But only with time and experience we understand how right grandparents are, and in general, the elderly who have gone through a greater number of situations.

Well, once, in one of my many life highlights, I began to think that life cannot be taught to be lived; it simply has to be lived.

NEW LIFE

The beginning of a new life story, I left behind all those wonderful experiences that helped me to grow and be who I am. In these moments I thank God and life itself for each one of the situations I experienced.

The best, having had the opportunity to live in the jungle, enjoy nature a totally different lifestyle from the one I had been living, all those wonderful people with whom I had the joy of sharing unforgettable moments, with many of whom nowadays we still talk, all those polygon courses, the roll call, learn to wear a rifle with a heavy uniform too much for a 45 kg. girl at that time, in boots which were even heavier, go through the mud, run, jump, etc. Experiences that I will keep forever; To know the other side of Colombia, to visit lands that I didn't even know they exist, the Malpelo majesty, traveling by ship several days, flying by helicopter more than an average Colombian, artillery will always be my favorite, taking wonderful pics throughout all those tours, which today are stored as the most valuable treasure in a great friend's house, to be delivered in a modest ceremony to my son when he is of age and he has his own space. His parents' history told in pictures, each one of those photos reflects that unconditional love that we had for a long time, a love that allowed me to leave a career, a company, friends, families, way of life, and many amenities and take the hard decision to go to his side to be with him and always be his support. Maybe it was wrong or maybe it was right, what really matters is what happened, what was experienced or that it never can be changed.

Continuing with life experience count, that school where I was, perhaps, where many don't have the opportunity to learn, has been the best school, and for sure it has been the best for me, because it's what I lived.

Everyone has their perception and tastes, everyone will see whether or not they're satisfied or happy with what they have lived, the truth, I give thanks for every one of the experiences I faced.

Each one decides how to face the situations of life, since there is a free will, and that is precisely what often makes us get out of our own way.

Well, now, after all, new goals have been set in my life already, and I hope to do my best to achieve them, that is precisely what gives us the satisfaction of living, the purposes, the goals, there's always a place where you want to arrive; In the beginning to move forward, try to don't leave unfinished tasks, it is healthier to evaluate the situation when it is no working and reorganize goals.

OLD DAYS' NOSTALGIA
AND TODAY'S JOY

Why deny it? When we remember the past, there is an occasional tear without thinking, so why we deny we have feelings that make us more human? I won't be an exception to the rule.

Of course I am nostalgic to remember all those moments full of true love, of tenderness, of fellowship that we share, I decided to remember the good things only, the positive, which is what really worth hold in the memory, the rest I threw it away already. All that mental junk's not good at all, because now I only think about build a life for my son full of as positive things as possible. If that actor in the famous movie "life is beautiful" could invent the best games to his little son in the middle of a war, why couldn't I?, what happened is water under the bridge; and I'm in the middle of a wonderful life, of course there are problems such as the poor economic situation, it isn't easy for a single mother and in spite of food quota my son's father collaborates with, it isn't easy to confront the situations that daily happen, I juggling, joint prayers, and even magic, to get ahead in one of the most expensive cities in our beautiful country. "No pain, no gain".

When I decided to settle in Cartagena, that familiar saying made more sense. It's a beautiful, quiet city, by the sea, and has a lovely history, walking in the night through the walled city is one of the most wonderful things I have ever seen. It has a special charm, the gentle breeze, the sea's fragrance, the colonial architecture, the old houses, those balconies with hanging plants, the houses' giant doors, the walls, the music at the squares, the candles on the tables outside the restaurants, all wrapped in overwhelming nostalgia in the good sense of the word, the crafts of the squares, the meetings I attend with a wonderful group of people who each day bring the most valuable experiences and life knowledge, art exhibitions, cruises that come and go and provide the city with a livelihood such as tourism, bays with yachts and boats anchored at the docks, during the day all that bustle full of history, the heat with a nice breeze, the busy streets of the city center where all daily activities must be done, or the neighborhoods of the edge, , all that charm and more, are for me the best of life.

Every moment lived has its charm and its beauty, what we like to remember produces well-being; that is what we must keep, the rest isn't worth it.

WONDERFUL DAYS

The same those await us all as we are giving a welcome to our lives.

It's a holiday, around seven in the morning, late for me because I wake up daily at four thirty; It is one of those which are in wonderful days' category, I get up, I make coffee, I go out to my house's terrace and Beethoven's fifth symphony is playing; my neighbor loves good music. The day is sunny, it's a warm morning, the trill of my neighbor's bird's collection it's a beautiful contrast. I take one of my books and I get to read a little in the best of environments; when the man of my life rushes, with his ruffled hair, still in pajamas, with sleepy eyes.

You can't imagine the feeling when that small piece of heaven hugs me; no more reading, no more coffee, and enjoying true love, kisses me with the most tender and sweet kisses in the middle of a hug a little awkward, a little abrupt and throws that the most touching word for me, "Mommyyyyy", at that moment everything is worth it, everything makes sense. Thank God, for this happiness!! Thanks for this joy that invades me and bristles me, all those feelings involve me in an ecstasy... and that day becomes the best day ever.

MY HALLMARK

I agree that everything we do, we do from the heart, we give that personal stamp on each thing and situation we undertake, that emotion of fixing the space where we live, of giving it functionality and at the same time that warmth to feel it a home, that empty space before, becomes everything for you after that, something we can be proud of, because we have achieved that and, in one way or another we are represented in it. That's beautiful and it isn't done in one day, it will take time to leave everything as I really want it.

To me, who love art in all its aspects, when you enter in my space you feel a full of history atmosphere, art, and it has a life of its own; paintings made for me especially, invaluable of course. A small and growing collection of all possible book themes are part of my most precious treasures; music, even if it's no longer used.... I love having my favorite artists' CDs. I'm a romantic, it hurts me to see how technology has been gradually moving things that have history and even life, like books. For me, to read in a tablet or computer it's not the same than take the book in my hands, the bookmarker..., for me to read is a big ceremony , it's a provision, a very special moment of my day, when I wrap myself in that universe and travel through it, I am cultivating In my baby that same taste for reading, I teach him every day how to take a book, how special it is, what it means, he has his own at his fingertips and looks at me, and even sits next to me with one of him to imitate me, I usually read him stories, I know that all these things have gone, they are not in fashion these days, the magic is over when we decide to take it out of our lives, the courtships with a letter, that furtive encounter, when day by day I was building a story, they have moved it to the cell phone, social networks.

In general, people don't even meet, and when they do it, is even funny to see them, everyone watching the phone, there are few moments when they talk, the meeting of friends of the university, those gatherings to catch up, they haven't done those any more, it's more by getting into a friend's virtual space there is no need to see him and sit down to enjoy his company, and little by little we are losing physical contact in relationships. Today we can see marriages breaking up and falling in love again by chat, and when they're in the same space they're completely ignored, I still don't know how to call it but it's a phenomenon that is spreading by leaps and bounds.

Children don't want to go to the park, for their parents it's more comfortable to buy them an electronic gadget or even a tablet for discarding, I'm not agree, my son is a stubborn but I am happy with whom he is, and I hope to share enough for him to prefer to talk to me face to face instead of sitting on the computer and isolating oneself from reality.

I want to play with my son as much as I can, see his laugh, enjoy his presence, that is achieved by being with him, sharing every moment, maybe I value this more because my work doesn't allow me to be with him all the time, and I get home late, exhausted, but my energies are magically recharged just thinking of a hug, a "Mommy" or that tender and sweet kiss, that's the best in my life.

Don't allow that in the hurry to make a living, life goes away. It's what often happens when we see people slaves of their work, in an office

until late at night, and coming home to finish what couldn't be done;
The best advice I can give, after all that I have experienced, is that life
is much more than that, it's much more to try… it's start doing, is to
take your own action, to claim what really belongs to you. The first
thing is to think about what we deserve and what we have, perhaps it
is a big difference between one concept and the other, but in any way,
we must self-assess what we are doing every day.

The most valuable things in life are those that we can't buy, those that
we forget that exist because we simply have them at our disposal and
as they don't have any cost for us, we stop valuing them as they are; a
sunset, a sunrise, the feeling of bare feet either in the grass or in the
sand or in the shore, feel the breeze, stop in the middle of the street
and just feel how other people run from one place to another, enjoy
the rain, dance in the middle of the storm, count stars, contemplate
the moon, breathe, feel your heartbeat, stop in the day and escape to
a place you enjoy, run aimlessly, even walk aimlessly, raise your hands
and give Thanks to heaven for being alive, for breathing, for feeling…
people who don't have all those privileges paradoxically are the most
grateful, is when I ask myself.: do we need lose to win?

Possibly so, and you have to stop complaining about what you don't
have and fully enjoy what you already have in order to move forward;
nature is perfect, when something doesn't work for us, it removes it.

It's like the snail which changes its house every time it's outgrowing;
I am sure that the snail, when it opens the house is not thinking of
a larger one, far less in having several houses in different colors. The
truth is we don't need anything we have or at least the large majority,
but consumerism drowns us in, it poisons us, it makes us sick.

I have friends with so many shoes, the day they wear them they get
crystallized and they leave them in the middle of the street, other keep
new clothes with labels for years, they have so much that they don't

get to wear everything they've bought, but just as if they had nothing; They buy a new outfit almost daily, that desire to fill that gap, that obsession for change to improve, there's no better change than those we make ourselves, in our way of facing life and its situations.

It takes a lifetime to do that, life is a valuable loan that sometimes we don't know how to make the most with it, as when they lend us a valuable book and for watching television or doing anything else we leave it anywhere and when we finally want to read it, the owner comes to have it back. Now imagine there is only one edition of that book and it's so valuable that there's no way to get it anywhere else, we are so busy in nothing, that we forget everything.

Enjoy the company of the people who is part of your life, those mentors that leave one or another teaching, positive things that we can treasure to grow and learn every day; stop keeping your eyes in your mistakes, stop trying to fix them, just enjoy their worth company and share life experiences, it will be useful for the most unlikely person; good works are okay as long as they aren't done looking for anything in return, giving without waiting is the most beautiful and rewarding thing in life, you shouldn't give away ... you should teach.

Don't look for, because you'll find, and most of the time it isn't what we like to find the most.

Love yourself before anyone else; value yourself so much that other people have to value you.

Be humble without confusing it with poverty, they're two very different things, and poverty will always be mental, the universe is so rich that it reaches everyone, what usually happens is that many people don't know how to take what they need.

Listen to the elders, and have respect for them; very soon (sooner than we expect or imagine) you will be in their condition.

Grow up, but keep that child in you, the one you keep in your heart, don't try to shut it up, it is the most beautiful thing you can have in your life, it's the same one that will play with your children and will be the one that will remind you how to enjoy your life.

Don't stop dreaming, remember...dreams come true, so make your dreams your life project, don't despair.

Meanwhile love, laugh, shout, dance, explode with all the possible emotions and enjoy them; don't think so much in the past or in the future, cause it's precisely what doesn't let you enjoy the present as it should be; don't lose your innocence and have the courage to love so many times as possible in life; go ahead even if you don't see the light at the end; listen carefully and then analyze; do your best always; don't keep anything useless, (including negative memories); when you feel able to leave everything and start over, do it at once and without fear, don't ask anyone for opinion or permission, it is your life; in the most difficult situations look for your true friends and family, but look for them in the best situations even more.

Dress according your mood, when you're sadder look for the happiest colors.

Learn from nature, share more with her, it will always have something beautiful to bring you, live every day without waiting for the next one, but with common sense enough to live the rest of your life.

Don't listen to gossip, read more than you watch television, watch your surroundings daily, seek to feed your spirit like taking care of your body, don't expect anything from anyone but give everything of yourself, smile at life, even if it's turning its nose, if she's bitter... laugh at her.

Take all the situations and put yourself in the task of getting the positive, everything has something positive, take those lemons and make yourself lemonade with the sugar of your soul.

Pay less attention of what people say, think about your own being, change what is really necessary, and forget about giving your opinion about what they haven't asked for.

Live intensely, do what you like more and bring it to excellence, quite possibly that's your dreams purpose.

The lessons that life leaves us are diverse, sharing them with wonderful people makes me feel privileged; in this regard, I just ask God that this lines reach the people, and one way or another leave a smile in their faces and a better mude.

CHAPTERS WITHOUT CLOSURE.

In an untold time of regrets, any friend among others, told me she has wanted to get ahead and get rid of a relationship that had finished and as a result, there were three wonderful children, she referred to him as the "$% # &". It had been time, four years to be exact, but the wounds hadn't healed yet, and listening to her talk about him was like as if he had just left her life. She didn't want to go to therapy because they could believe her crazy, I asked her: baby, what's the point of continuing getting your life bitter for anything that it's only in your mind?

You've realized that he's happy without you, and instead, you... a beautiful, talented, professional, excellent mother, who is still denying the opportunity to give your heart a new breeze, and all this thanks to what? To that resentment that you still have in your heart, since that day when he decided stop sharing his life with you.

She cries of rage, what a shame, at least, we're in her apartment room, that new apartment her father bought her shortly after the separation; a new apartment, but full with the furniture that was part from the old home. That vent moment, as I was close to her, it meant a lot to me. She had a sip of water and breathes; I passed her a tissue, of those that I always carry in my wallet because I'm a whiny. Here I am, making myself strong, to give strength to this woman that God put me on the road, I already said a little calmer: "Baby, for some reason you and I are having this conversation, I am not a psychiatrist, nor a psychologist or a therapist, I am a woman who like you, has been through the heartbreaking pain of a separation, all I can tell you is my point of view of this situation, and just because you're asking me, but life taught me something as I passed for those stormy hours, and it was that there isn't anyone in the world who can help you, or a magic pill, to overcome something, if your brain and your feelings don't allow it, your children are already adults, you are going to be a grandmother in a short time, at this point if you feel you don't want to go on, that's what you will get, four years have passed by, and I can see that you still speak about him with hate, and if you come across his new partner I think you are able even to kill her in an act of anger and intense pain. It's time to overcome this and keep going, because the only one harmed is you.

She confesses to me lowering her gaze, and sobbing, that she always hated her, just for the sake of being with him, and she would have hated anyone who took that place.

She didn't hate her as she thinks, in fact she hated herself, and everything she couldn't be, and she saw herself reflected in that woman 15 years younger than her.

Actually, doing numbers from when they started their relationship is not the important thing, the main thing is when you decide to overcome it and when is not going to harm you anymore, because you can't move forward with that hate load: "she is younger than me, slimmer, taller, I feel less, sometimes I wonder if he left me because I'm fat"; she look down.

I look at her beautiful face and catch her eyes to say: "nobody leaves anyone" we are human beings, we aren't anyone's owners, the fact of sharing our life or some moments with someone we chose, it isn't a guarantee that they will be ours forever. I think that relationships have to be built, day by day, minute by minute, we are the product of what we think, if you keep so much toxic things in your mind, at some point, your body will also reflect that. You must debug, leave behind, but it's your unique and exclusive decision, from nobody else.

And without thinking, he reproaches: "...and my children, I think of my children... he is their father!"

To which I respond: "And that's going to last forever, that can't be changed, because instead of seeing everything dark and gray, look at the positive side: your ex-husband is happy, and therefore he transmits that happiness to your children, each time they are together, the woman who accompanies him, whoever she is, treats them well, and that's a gain, she is clear in they are the man she loves' children, if at any time, that man comes to your life with whom you decide to start a story, ask yourself, if you would be able to get to have something with someone who doesn't love your children. Your children will matter, no matter how big they are or if they have their own lives, for a mother it'll always be important how they treat their children, that they don't displace them, or go out with rudeness.

The other thing you should check, is that story you had with him, however it was, and how hard it was, is just a story right now. Only you have the power to live remembering every fragment of your past, of that story, and living in the past, re-victimizing yourself, again and again, sometimes it becomes that drug, feeling pain for the same, y share it to each one next to you, you decide till where you will keep carrying with you that heavy load.

The doorbell rings, and we both look at the door, she gets up and answers the door, at that moment, I look at her apartment, which is new but with old furniture, and I imagine a person coming out of the mud, letting her dirty body dry a little and dressing new clothes on. It's necessary if we want to overcome stages, do a deep cleaning of everything to move forward.

I reminded myself how much I love photography and that I even filled a five hundred pictures album. Those photos treasure the story of my first husband, my son's father, and it seemed selfish to want to break them. I think that belongs to my son.

I created new accounts in social networks, I reinvented myself, the more it hurt, the more I felt I was surpassing him, I started from scratch everything. But my son is the fruit of that story that reminds me that it worth it. I couldn't ever deny that he's an exemplary father, and for some reason I chose him to be my partner, but life is teaching us that facing situations, we must evolve, and keep going with or without the people we believed would be beside us, whatever happens, life goes on.

Because refusing the opportunity to move on, refusing to be happy, refusing to evolve, and finding our self's best version, are the questions that will always be in my head. Sometimes all we need is determination and decision-making power, we blame life, and the whole world for what happens, but in the end, the real guilty is oneself, since life can't be lived by someone else, we make up stories, we create movies to make us feel like the victims, and that inspires pity in people around us, the same pity is increased again and again by that need to live in that vicious circle. Is like continuing to open the wounds every day, and get ripped them until they bleed again, and continue doing that forever.

I read in some book that everything that happens to us is attracted to ourselves, it's a way of seeing things, what works for you, or what makes you feel better, it'd be excellent that the topic of mental health weren't a taboo, the service should be provided from childhood to adults seeking to improve life's quality, there are issues that can be treated in time avoiding mental catastrophes, people's death who don't see a way out or a psyche's strengthen. It'd be a purpose from the classrooms, focused on life's education. Developed countries have advanced the subject already, and they have professionals in life training, turning the psychological issue around, helping in this way more ordinary people without much effort; but with all the accessible technology we have this days, researching, documenting and adopting behavior changes in order to end devastating situations, it's new era's bonus which we could take advantage of.

In another run into this woman, in a completely different environment, I felt her more relaxed, with another spirit, another tone, she was well-dressed and with another countenance, we restart the closing chapters subject, I asked her why after so many years she was not able to take her and ex-husband's photos off from social networks yet; so she answered, "they are part of a story"

Are you really interested in keeping opening that past story which also caused you so much pain, now in your present? I asked; don't you think that you are venerating him and paying tribute to whom is not anymore?

I insist, it's your decision, it's your way of thinking, but if you are asking me for advice and my point of view, that's precisely the one I give you with all the love I have in my heart. If you think it should be the children's legacy, you have your right of don't start a new story, leave that profile for them if you consider that for respect to them you shouldn't wipe it away, as I told you. These are ways to see things, but if I'm sure, as long as you keep hammering the wound, it'll never heal.

She answers me: What if is some part of me that I don't want to let go?

I replied: In that case you must analyze everything very well. As long as you continuing ruin your moments thinking about what has happened and tormenting yourself again and again for what once was, but nowadays not, life won't return you time; instead of lamenting and blaming others you must be at the helm, and turn it one hundred and eighty degrees if necessary, no looking back, without regrets, you alone are the responsible of how you feel, so don't allow yourself to grow old being bitter, and complaining. The body reflects what the heart keeps, there are lots of clinical studies about it, and it isn't about physical beauty, since this slipped like water through the fingers, no, you aren't always twenty years old, it's more about inner peace and pure soul, reflecting calm and a transparent aura, that's your covering letter in front of people doesn't know you eyes.

We are energy, so when we relate each other, that's what we feel between humans and living beings. There are people with such a heavy energy that when they arrive at a house... even the cactus dies!

TO BE A MOM OR NOT TO BE, THAT'S THE QUESTION!

There are so many souls and bodies in the world so it seems absurd to classify them, or include them in profiles; however, psychologists and psychiatrists are dedicated to analyze specific behaviors and reactions, to avoid situations or to help evolve people who need it.

That's very respectable. What today after so many vicious circles we call the (long-awaited) mental health, in this era where technology captures us, where it's easy to know the whole world in less than an hour; thanks to social networks and the Internet, is another story, and everyone lives it depending on their virtual reality, beauty stereotypes have transcended to the stereotypes of perfect or ideal life, and intangible values have been left behind so we replace them with numbers in bank accounts, in this same big or small world depending on the perspective from where is looked, thousands of stories come and go simultaneously; and it's here, in the middle of my now, where I analyze each person in the cafe where I am, and among many memories of real women who, one way or another, have been through my life, some as shooting stars, others by long periods of time, and likewise those that are still part of the lines I daily write, I think that between the most difficult and complicated questions for a woman throughout her life , is to make the decision to be a mother.

Since it's so complex and implies the total and real detachment of a part of its own, there are many things and situations which you have to give up at that time, depending on how it's contemplate, we're human beings and we're not perfect, however speaking with so many women the only thing in common was that each single one of them tried to lead a perfect lifestyle, and after all, there are difficult things and impossible things for us.

When I decided to be a mother I realized you always are criticized: for good, for evil and just in case.

After several years with my son, I understood that the only thing that really matters is that he can receive well-being and let him be independent enough to face society, but with limits to don't reach debauchery.

There's the successful and middle age woman, who doesn't dare to be a mother yet, because she hasn't got a partner. There is a very graphic film, called Plan B, where they showed that the important thing is what that woman wants in her life, as long as we have the tools to be happy and we use them, this same happiness will be spread to all, it's not about living a lifetime looking for happiness outside, when the way to face situations it's something inherent in a being, as difficult as they seem, what we cannot control must be released so it can flows and in this way won't harm us. Once is outside us, it's much easier to go on.

On the other hand, there's the woman who decided by conviction, and not for any other reason, don't be a mother. Because she isn't interested at all, she thinks how her life is going and she enjoys it, perfect! It's respectable.

There's also the one who yearn to be financially free and remain focused on it, forever and ever. She has no time for anything other than making money, have a coffee becomes business and her only joy's a closed deal. She lives absorbed by her accounts, working to give herself the lifestyle she deserves, although she doesn't have to pay for it. She sees the relationships with a dollar sign as well, what this person does provide to her life which can be translated into money?, and she lives gaining material things trying to fill the great emotional hole, which she has created by her own.

Then the forty's arrive and the priorities change, now the race's against the clock, she invests everything and more to look younger or to stop the time, that begins to charge in every inch of her skin all those unhappy situations, all those frustrations. She didn't enjoy what she had, because she was thinking about what she wanted.

There is also the single mother who, in spite of everything, decided to have her son, against the odds, with her head up high, even every time she fall behind a payment, or feel that the responsibility is overwarming. However a toddler's kiss is enough to keep going, and get your best and show your best smile to start every day.

Cases and more cases, among others, the lady over forty's almost in her fifty's, almost a grandmother to be, who by thinking a lot, managed living in a bad marriage for too many years, and in the end, life itself ends up taking the decision which she feared that much and waited so long, for which he trembled every time she wanted to send everything where it belonged, and today at his age, she sights and self-claims for don't have done it so much earlier, she worries for the people around her more than for herself, she put so much up because of her children, with fear that one day they would hold that against her, and paradoxically they are the ones who have their lives far away from her nowadays.

There is the widow who at same age as the previous one, is in a very similar situation, both holding grudges in their hearts, and likewise, both have the right to try again and start all over, it just depends on themselves.

I couldn't miss the twenty-year-old who dreams of a huge wedding, and a fairy tale. She's frustrated because her family often asks her how soon is going to happen. If there was a life manual where they anticipate that no one should be worried about what people think or say, the world would be much better, however, it's proven that there are people who no matter how many times they are told, prefer getting burnt and even die trying. We should thank them for the examples that have been remained somewhere in history.

I could write and write until my fingers were numb; however, I wouldn't finish sharing the stories. I shall just refer to the one who in one way or another echoed in my life.

And here I am, sitting on my apartment´s terrace, enjoying a beautiful sunset and the home made coffee taste, writing these lines struggling a little bit with occasional mosquitoes because of the Caribbean weather, interrupting me sometimes to the point of bites, but the sunset is worth it.

I am and I will always be an inveterate romantic, sick of love, and with sweet sweat that's why mosquitoes like me so much.

Well, after a busy afternoon and full of commitments, I arrive at my home to follow these lines inspired by a mother's job.

As I wrote before, there are just a few stories that marked my life which I'll tell at some point, but now I remember a very special one, it seems that in the past generation, it was very common in families to have more than one heir, perhaps because the prosperous economy, because contraception methods weren't widespread, or because society pressed, and people let themselves be pressured, when the first baby arrived, they said, "Wouldn't you like having the sibling?" when the second arrived, and if was as the same sex as the first, "you have to look for the girl or the boy", and if they had one of both, they said "Aww.. but the boy needs a little brother", I have heard so many stories, and I'm not sure whether it's because of social pressure or another reason, but at that time it was very common to have more than one child. The truth is children are a great bless, but they must be brought with a big responsibility to this ruin world.

The life's conditions get worse, but the main thing is our decision. Knowing urban stories and myths, I discovered that there are women able to get pregnant for money… and live from it, either to retain a job, taking advantage of the women and children rights' legal loopholes, using any ruse to stay at home and become the victim and the martyr in front of society's eyes. Or for "retaining" a partner who doesn't want to be besides her any more, and giving time to a relationship that honestly doesn't work.

There are so many troubles and there are all kinds of foundations and entities in charge of this particular issue.

Hopefully, at school and at educational entities, they will teach deeply about bringing a child to this world's responsibility. I think we would avoid many headaches.

They should teach that people can't be bought, they must be conquered, and this way, they would recover extraordinary values that could allow more conscious and less dependent society.

Just as a young, beautiful, intelligent, hardworking, responsible woman can depend on what will they say, what people thinks about it, as what she decides to do with her life is very respectable, questions are arise: would be the same determinations taken, if there weren't the feared "what will they say"? Or they would take a completely different road?

Perhaps without social pressure, the decisions of thousands of women would be other, perhaps even when that society is already accepting a few more same-sex couples, there are still people who take a certain journey, until they stay alone and refuse the opportunity to be happy with someone else...because of society... but these are my assumptions, "me and my better world's ideal", kinder, more human, full of love, and with more self-esteem that wasn't definitively enough for many people, who never managed to love and accept themselves.

LIFE HISTORIES

At a museum somewhere in Cartagena, there was a sculpture exhibited, of one piece of wood, with which the artist succeed making an only one breast's bust. In front of this piece of wood, I had a magical moment where my emotions surfaced from my life story, it was very touchy, I sighed, I looked at the sky and thanked God because at least I could breathe and still live, something that I once yearned for. I think that breathe is as wonderful as feel life, everything that encompasses that breath system's so wonderful that there are medicine books only about this subject, however, for those of us who have the joy of doing it daily, becomes imperceptible, so normal that we even do it wrong.

The sculpture reminded me that I'm still alive despite the physical and psychological mutilation that I suffered several years ago. That sculpture was mutilated, and could be interpreted as a lady's breast, or a heart... They mutilated me both of them, and nevertheless, I'm still alive, although I don't deny at that time I thought I would die, it was the positive attitude what saved me, I make this clear, it was the way I looked at my day by day, and how I was processing to the most difficult situations of my life, to turn them around and overcome it. All this proves that feelings despite being mutilated in the cruelest way and without anesthetics, they can recover and revive.

Today everything has a completely different perspective, I'm no longer the girl who cried inward and was showing the happiness mask, now I consider myself a transparent woman, because I don't need to hide anything, I live my life, I enjoy it, in spite of everything and everyone, it's the only thing I have, and is borrowed, until it's my time to leave, and with how this uncertainly world is... it could be today, or maybe tomorrow.

THE PARADOXES OF LIFE

In Cartagena's down town, at the "ciudad amurallada" more specifically, it's ten past eleven in the morning at the beginning of December of any year, it's a sunny day with a warm breeze that plays with my freshly brushed hair, the hustle of this deafening place, the crowd walks with care, with no hurry which characterizes the tourists in these times, and suddenly starts to rain, without warning, not a single sign that the downpour was coming so I soaked from head to toes, I felt so small, so little thing i front of nature's majesty, while everyone was running looking for a dry and secure place, I walked slowly, drenched, happy and delighting in every drop of water.

There won't be enriched feeling, and that made me feel millionaire, since there are places in the world where people would give everything just to experience that warm falling rain's sensation.

I think that every place has its own charm and each moment is unique and unrepeatable.

If we wait for that perfect moment, I think we would waste our life trying to find that perfection that surely only exists in our mind, that's why a few years ago, I decided to take every one of my moments and make them perfect, that's what it is, to enjoy life, feel me alive, never stop being children in our heart, to be able to live without fear and with the certainty that the only moment we have is the one we are living right now.

You can't live in parallel; if we keep our minds busy thinking about solving our world, or in situations we create in our minds, maybe looking for predict what never is going to happen. Is something like create a problem just to solve it, just in case it happens.

I have tried to put my mind blank many times but I end up reaching the same conclusion as always, and it's that there is too much wonder in this world to waste it, and is enough with the hours we should sleep because our human condition, if it was for me I wouldn't sleep, I feel I have too many books to read, too many places to visit, too many coffees to drink, too many friends to talk to, too many sports to practice, too many stories to write, and maybe... why not? Recreate them too.

OF THE ESSENCE AND OTHER STEREOTYPES

We are at the time when everyone is categorized! We all have been stereotypes' victims which humanity maybe creates to feel unique or equal, like others, or for anything else.

I don't agree with that thing of living life looking for a style between thousands of styles. In my childhood I was the girl who looked like a boy, because I never identified with dolls, I only used them to tear them apart or cut their hair. I did my first transplants to them; Do you believe that? But I always lived pending what toy my cousin had, since his toys were really interesting, such as cars and the super track where they were driving by they self, the long-awaited tricycle; we were fighting all the time because obviously I wanted to drive it not be a passenger, and since at that age I was taller than him, I always came out ahead. The blocks and legos were my favorites.

But they usually gave me things like a plastic kitchen set, which ended in its box because it never caught my attention, or a kitchen... It must be why I was never interested in cooking, until it became a necessity.

They even gave me once a broom and a mop, and my grandmother was pissed off because I ended up on the top of the mop like a cowgirl competing in a race with my cousin, who had a stick horse that was practically the same.

It's wrong to frustrate a child that much with those kinds of toys by classified them in a stereotype that only exists in some retrograded and gridded parents minds. The truth is I tried not to affect me, but at that age everything affects, and the small things are so big, but the story didn't end there, the clothes issue was the worst, they forced me to wear cheesy dresses that I hated, they looked like an umbrella, and with the Cartagena's heat, where I lived my childhood, the shorts were better to climb and sneak into the trees, of course, but at that time the fact that a girl, who should be feminine or look like a fairytale princess, was climbing on a tree was inconceivable, and even more for me since I was raised by my grandparents.

I loved bicycles, but only until I could afford one, I could finally learn to ride it, because under their yoke that was unthinkable, so I couldn't learn how to swim, or to ride skates since they overprotected me so much that they didn't let me live that stage that will never return.

If my grandmother who still lives and my grandfather if he lived, found out everything I have done, I think they wouldn't stand it, to climb with a rope through the walls of a tall building, or to have sailed for so many days on a full of men's ship, to have trained alongside a marine's battalion, to have eaten mud (literally) going into the thick Pacific jungle... my grandmother would be infarcted and my grandfather would return to life and died again,

They also haven't discovered that I received military training and shoot practically all weapons, even ship cannons, that I had the opportunity as well to learn how to sail, and why not one day go skydiving; for some reason the world evolves more every day, and I try to don't make the same mistakes with my son, he must be free to be happy, and I let him know it's a life's choice and so he shouldn't be restricted by any family member who believes that have the right to decide for him.

The ideal as parents is act as that life example for the children, being mentors and guides in what can be done. This is it... if not, the world wouldn't be world.

BETWEEN BITTER AND SWEET

If everything were sweet, it wouldn't have any grace, maybe the flavors are only mind's inventions product of thousands of years of experiences of others. Each one interprets things' taste as we consider it; for example, I like the strong coffee, without sugar; another woman can try it and say that it's the most bitter and unpleasant thing she has tasted, because she always drinks coffee with milk and she sweetens it. Of course it will taste completely different of mine, but... Who are we to judge others? Or... Who are we to get into the tastes of others? Everyone should learn to enjoy their own coffee without wondering what the other think and why it will be prepare in one way or another. If each person get focus into their coffee and try all the coffee styles until they get their favorite, it would be a happiest world.

I personally love the coffee according to my mood, the weather, and the nonsense there is inside my head; I love coffee in all its presentations, and I enjoy it as if I was drinking my last one. That is my life philosophy, many years ago I adopted it after I had the opportunity to continue in this world, and since then, I live every moment as if It was the last one, maybe that's why I enjoy them so much.

Every moment that I live, I think it worth it being lived, and I wouldn't like using a time machine, just because I'm not interested in changing anything.

Recently I saw a movie that touched my heart, where the principal actor was able to see her future, and being perfectly able to change it, to avoid the suffering that the loss of her only daughter meant, but she surprisingly decided that it was more important to have her, and enjoy her motherhood and everything that led to the premature loss; so she didn't change anything and lived even more intensely every moment with her baby, knowing that she could enjoy it just for a short time.

Humanity arrives to this world with only one sure thing, and is that sooner or later, it will end up dying. However we all live avoiding the issue and many of us are so attached to all this, that we don't realize is a gift, enjoyable, with expiration date.

They should teach us those principles in school, which really are basic and simple and I think we would live more conscious, more awake, and therefore, happier. It would be all easier.

WHAT YOU LIKE MOST

We are in an era where everyone lives stuck with technology. Many years ago at school, the teacher sent us homework about making an essay about how the technology development it would be in the future. I still remember my teacher didn't like the job, he told me that I was too divergent in my thinking, but the truth is he was right, and time proved that, what happens is that nobody wanted or imagined what is really happening today.

Technology is getting out of hand, and it will get worst, but it's up to each one to put limits and regain our healthy habits so we won't get out of control.

I always was the different girl, the one who starts discussions with the teachers and who preferred to go to the library to read rather than enjoy the recess. I wish we could do what we really like in the schools, I wish we could choose the competencies we are interested in, after having basis, of course, and to be able to choose what to do in those hours that become our whole world and a great part of our life.

I think a whole life is not enough to get the level of knowledge and learn all the things I like. Perhaps life is too short to be complicated, and every day is a new opportunity to be happy and make everything go well, something like a start over with a clean slate.

If universities teach a little beyond academics, we'd have happier generations, doing what they really like and not what they must.

There are lots of people who venture into a university career and at a half of it they realize that it wasn't what they really wanted, the worst of all is that they keep going, and they finish it and they also work in it and are fully unhappy for the rest of their working life.

Likewise, when young couples join in marriage, and after few years they realize that wasn't the person with whom they would like to spend the rest of their lives, however, they continue for a lifetime involved in a sad relationship, just because the relationships needs two halves and if one of both is not at ease, the other therefore ends in one way or another being completely unhappy.

If we dedicate ourselves in soul, body, heart and life to experience what attracts our attention and also identify what we really like, everyone would live in constant look for what they really feel comfortable doing, there would be more kindness in all services, and people will work with true passion.

In this way the days weren't strenuous and nobody would arrive home tired, and I speak of that fatigue where you want to send everything to where is no return; that chronic exhaustion, where you don't know if you are hungry, thirsty, want to run away or simply passing out at the house entrance, so that a family member arrives and picks up what you left of yourself.

There will always be a reason to move on and continue with a victorious air, with the taste of what is lived, at last and after all, no one can live for you, and nobody is going to feel your satisfaction, it's personal, and not transferable.

In the same way if we fale at some point, as is natural, life goes on, even if it sounds cruel, the world keeps turning and everything follows a course; we're so small and we are part of the whole; Why we don't live doing what we really enjoy? Happiness is within each one, what happens is, that most haven't been taught to be aware of it, and spend their lives in the happiness search, believing that it depends on one or another factor, and the saddest thing is that only at the end most discover where happiness really comes from, when it's already too late, when there's no going back, and as well there're also those who never realize and die without knowing it, believing that it depended on everything but themselves.

..AND I FACED MY PAST

Few days ago, I had the bravery, the bravery women feel in the ovaries.

Charged with a lot of courage, and with the best attitude, scissors in one hand, and a handkerchief in the other, just in case, and on my apartment terrace, with the sea of witness and the scenery of the stage; I got comfortable, and I prepared myself to face the seven albums that contain five hundred or seven hundred photos. My whole life is there, besides that in each photograph had written few words to tell a story. After so many books read and so many therapies, about overcoming pain, how to face it and get ahead, I decided that seven years after, the perfect moment had finally arrived, (according to my intuition), to face this great challenge, I can't deny that when I saw the first album I only took the photos that I decided to keep In my life, those that produced me joy, a merely positive feeling, those which I considered that were deserved to be preserved; one by one was evaluated without much thought.

Incredible! But after nine hours in a row in which I only stopped for physiological needs, my history, more than fifteen years, had been reduced to a shoebox. I blessed the rest of them, I released them and freed myself, and I'd take the time to organize them in a new album.

It was more liberating exercise than boxing training, which was recommended to me by a mental health professional a few years ago. Incredibly with so little, I learnt so much, and I understood that everything I pass through, I would pass it all over again.

In these moments, I wouldn't change anything, I'd accept each one of those experiences and love them as much as my past, to let them go where they belong, with all they valuable life teachings, welcome my wonderful present, which I enjoy to the fullest.

The person I was, at that time, did what I consider fair, correct, since according to my potential it was what I could give, what I could react and do; that person has already evolved and continues evolving every day.

It cost me so much to turn on that famous saying of my grandfather, "each day has enough troubles of its own".

From that moment when I finally had the courage and the bravery to face my past, everything changes. Maybe I unconsciously felt that keeping those memories didn't let me went completely out of that circle of pain that I created in my mind, or maybe I even felt that in the earthly plane there was a bond as strong as that emanating from those photos which kept that entire burden. We are energy, and inanimate things are also charged with energy, therefore if this balance is broken, there are energy failures, better known as negative energies. The studies say that we must balance the energies to reach that state of harmony, so longed for by human beings; this whole issue opened my eyes, and woke up to the possibility that my energies, now more aligned, flow with more proportion.

I once read that what we feel in the heart is what we end up attracting to our lives.

In one of my frequent visits to the bookstore, I stumbled upon a book called "The magic of order", and when I opened it I found a page in it that counts how keep in your life what you really love; the paragraph I read was precisely the one about photos organization, coincidence or not it wasn't very liberating, as the author says that there must be an order to clean and organize and the photos are practically the last item. However, for me, as it was a pending task, I needed several cups of coffee, and a lot of attitude to finally achieve it

This book ended up captivating me so much that I also did the exercise with the library, the most precious thing for me, however, I ended up making a very careful selection of books, and I kept the most important ones, the ones I reread, and I know, because I know myself, at some point I will reread them again.

I filled four book's boxes, which I send to a second hand bookstore and I ended up negotiating, they didn't give me much money for them, and the truth is that wasn't the point of my exercise, however, for me, the most valuable of all, is that I gave those books the opportunity to be read again, appreciated and valued, as much as I did, I also gave them the opportunity to share all those emotions, and valuable lessons of each one of them.

I realized that I even kept books that I made with my university's note books. I have always been very organized, and I had them very well detailed, each one of the diploma courses, certificates, updates, all that academic material, that since I studied it in their moment, I didn't even check them, which means that the knowledge was really assimilated.

I realized that I had everything stored in files of my brain's computer, so I began to investigate among my contacts, who would need any of these documents, and surprise! in a single day, I filled two more academic book's boxes that, I know, they will be great help and support to those people who are keeping them.

These experiences were really liberating.

Then I faced my wardrobe, I am creative, and everyone believes that I have lots of clothes and accessories, but for surprise of many, my wardrobe is quite austere, is only that everything is matching differently every time. Go shopping is not my favorite activity, it stresses me out have to do it, and I prepare myself with a check list, which I intend to get in a single day, and incredibly most of the times I get it entirely. I'm not a fashionista, rather I impose my own, and when I realize several people are using my crazy combinations, those that don't match or look bad; but I dress more to my feelings agreement and for encourage myself than for anything else, that's why my style is unique, and although they want to look the same the essence is only mine.

With this entire book thing, take out a lot of clothes that didn't make me happy, and I was wearing it just because it was in my wardrobe.

I was able to analyze, and it was true, the times I wore those clothes my attitude wasn't the same, and I decided to take them out of my life; I donated them. This exercise was also so liberating, my mood became much more cheerful and positive, all my energy was potentiated… and I still have to do the rest.

How good this exercise is, that I feel the need to do it with the whole house!!??

INTERRUPTED CHILDHOOD

With all this photos, many memories even from childhood were activated, those times where my worries weren't the same as now, nor the same of any boy or girl my age, I worried about having enough time in the recess to finish reading that history book's chapter, or metaphysics. It's curious that only until a few years ago I began reading novels, which I always considered a waste of time, how wrong I was, the novels brought inspiration to my life.

I still remember that I started reading them at university, and in the long turns at E.D., when the universe conspired and everything was filled with a false calm, I took advantage of reading those short novels, from then I put a little more into the surreal and idealistic world of novels, novels lead you to dream, that's why they are so addictive, however of the fifteen customary monthly books I read, only one is a novel.

My childhood was quite austere, I grew up with my maternal grandparents, and a come and go of cousins and family members all year long, I remember my grandfather's stories, about the Bermuda Triangle for example, he had a great ease of doing poetry, and I delighted in his gatherings, with no public, never interested in capturing that art somewhere, he considered that he didn't have enough talent to make it public, that same grandfather who also had an unparalleled talent to take out of a piece of wood the more beautiful figures, the manger was built by him and looked like expensive figures, of those unique ones there wasn't found in the country.

My negotiating spirit, since I remember, was to encourage him to write and find a way to publish it, sadly he died before trying. He was my tender father, my grandmother was very hard on me, until just a few years ago she let me hug her for the first time and kiss her, since I have memory, she didn't allow it, for respect. She went to extremes, it always was what she considered and it wasn't negotiable. I remember my gifts were chose as they wanted, for example a broom, a rag, a doll, a pot set, kitchens, but they gave my cousin toys that I always considered real toys, like cars, a Lego box, everything to make houses, buildings, airplanes, boats, etc.

Once in Christmas the best of all toys arrived: a tricycle, of course it was for my cousin, but my crying was so strong that I think I convinced them that if they left me the tricycle I wouldn't die asphyxiated in my own crying. From then on with the tricycle came a thousand fights to share this toy rights; I love my cousin, he's like my brother, but at that time I wanted to be stronger than him to be able to grab his attractive toys. At that moment the love for working out was born, my toys were different, my dolls ended up disarmed and I practiced my first transplants. Everything that had to do with the kitchen I swapped it with a friend; her parents had a grocery store, I preferred sweets than that useless junk.

I liked a game the most: the supermarket, there's where my business attitudes began, I was happy counting the money; I realized that our childhood is what really marks who you will become.

So today I am a mother, I try to give my son that freedom to play with what he considers is fun, after all, games shouldn't be about sexual identity, children are children, and the fact that he likes some toys more than others doesn't define his sexual identity, this is defined at a later stage, thank God the world has evolved and all those theories have already been reevaluated based on studies.

From childhood memories, I have always spoken loudly, when I was little, it seemed that I was screaming all the time, and it was very annoying for my grandparents, who took the parents role, they always told me to shut up, today I understand why I speak until you are blue in the face, and if they cover my mouth I literally get subtitled... for some reason I write.

I felt during all that time that they wouldn't let me express myself, that is why today I love the fact of standing in front of many people and expressing my point of view, and precisely that tone of voice that at some point in my life was annoying, today the same strong voice tone is my strength when speaking in public.

I was frustrated for many years by my voice tone, and then when I worked in sales I got the most out of it, and I keep taking it out.

Another of the precious memories of my childhood is that I was a weak girl...so to speak, I had asthma, all my childhood and adolescence, when I had the means I practiced a homeopathic treatment that managed to heal me. As I suffered asthma attacks, I was terrible at sport, the most serious of all was that gave me hypoglycemia attacks as well, which at that time had no relevance, but my body began to show the dreaded diabetes symptoms that was developed years later.

When it was time for physical education, maybe it was psychological, but I always got sick, and besides that, I felt very bad because I was different from all my classmates. I was born with a special condition in my joints. I have joint hyperlaxy. It's a condition that makes the whole body looks like rubber when stretched, in my time it was very rare, it was only seen at the circus, and people associated it with phenomenon and mockery, so when I squirmed to do some exercise my classmates made fun of me, it wasn't easy to try to do exercise when the teacher encouraged me and the rest of the class didn't stop laughing. However, this condition led me to strengthen my character and have the ability to take on the challenge despite the teasing and murmuring.

I can still writhe on my own axis, it seems I'd have fractured each day, and my limbs, since they have that condition, I used to lift weights to strengthen my muscles, and stay healthy challenging diabetes.

I learned to know my body in such a way that I provide what it asks me and I need and today I keep laboratory levels away from the diabetes condition, although I know that without discipline to stay healthy would be another story.

In my way I decided to run, for personal challenge rather than competition, as I love the exercise, for how it makes me feel, I practice several disciplines depending on the time and space I can dedicate.

Today I still keep in touch with my classmates, all lived experiences are enriching, and in one way or another I recognize that without those teasing, today I wouldn't have this personality; without all those experiences it wouldn't be the same, and very surely I would face life from a completely different perspective, or even rougher... maybe I wouldn't be alive.

I'm convinced that what we experience every time, is part of a whole we are building little by little, depending on how we take it makes a difference, nobody can live anyone's life, we can't live our father's or our children's life, each one is his own destiny's architect, therefore we must conscientiously analyze how we're carrying our work, and if we really feel happy with the progress. It's a job that only finishes when we leave this borrowed material body, while we keep it in the best or worst conditions we can and want, each one decides.

The important thing is about feeling good and on the right path, as long as we are conscious of it, there's the possibility of changing everything.

THE RELATIVITY OF A WONDERFUL TIME

We hear that time is relative very often, consciously or unconsciously we realize this type of messages, "one minute, but under water", we know it isn't the same.

We're aware time passes by, according to our perception, that's why when we do pleasant activities; it's different than when we do unpleasant ones.

Recently I heard an entrepreneur says: "I work like this now because in the future I want to be focus in what I like the most, be with my dogs, and move to the countryside... ". When I heard that, I really felt sorry, I had the perception he was dedicating all his efforts to live badly, and also sick, with a terrifying frenetic life that at any time it can collapse. We want to send that kind of orders to our brain to go against our human nature and give us that super human's connotation. Our essence will always be the same, we are human beings, and we can't fight against that.

There is a false thought of nothing is enjoyable and depends on each one to choose one path or another. For me there are non-negotiable things, such as my time, for example, for some years I made the decision to "work to live" and not "live to work", being very selective in what I do as well, I do what I really love, like and enjoy, in case it doesn't meet my expectations, I take it out of my life, and I reassess the situation immediately.

Thanks to all this, I feel that I live every day with the emotion that it deserves.

Few years ago my life changed completely and I woke up, I felt a rebirth like the Phoenix, it's precisely my current conviction and for that reason I work daily on that... in my self-knowledge.

That it's perhaps the most arduous human being task: to know, learn to tolerate, love and respect yourself in order to emanate that out and attract all that good energy back to you.

Since I referred to the Phoenix, I want to tell you the myth, there are several stories and I want to share the one I like the most of all:

The Phoenix was the only animal who was capable of resisting temptation in Eden, thereby earning eternity. Whatever version of its history we read, we will understand that this fantastic being symbolizes the same in every culture: immortality and resurrection.

Its origin goes back to Libya and Ethiopia, although its name comes from the Greek and means red.

Represented as a huge bird engulfed in flames and plumage like the fire, it was considered a demigod, as it was consumed by the flames and then reborn from its ashes.

This bird had deliciously scented feathers and was a sacred animal that, according to Herodotus, Pliny the Elder and Epiphany of Salamis, it only existed in Egypt. Every five hundred years it flew to the Heliopolis altar, where it burned and reborn the next day.

It was called Bennuy and symbolized the Nile's floods, the resurrection, and the sun, which dies and reborn every day.

In the early Christian tradition, the Phoenix lived in the Garden of Eden. When Adan and Eve were expelled, the angel who banished them sent off a spark from his sword that caught fire the bird's nest, making it burn until consumed; but as was the only beast that had refused to taste the forbidden fruit, immortality was conceived through the ability to be reborn from its ashes.

I love this story and curiously the animal with which I identify is the Eagle, the curious thing is that Phoenix mythology is compared to the Eagle.

I have taken every positive point of every situation of my life, and I have dedicated myself to make a count of the most significant ones in search of learning.

AMONG FRIENDS, SISTERS, PARTNERS OF LIFE, CHATS AND OTHER FOOLNESS

In one of many of my reflection moments, I began to think, how many friends go through our lives and how many of them stay forever?

I conclude that it's a personality matter.

I'm one of these people who love to treasure friendships, moments, soul memories instead of treasure material things, which eventually become deteriorated and fill us... but with garbage.

We are imperfect humans full of many noises, and the fact of achieving empathy with some other human being is already a gain.

Many people have passed by the course of my life, and there are of all kind: those that stay forever, those ones who are a learning and leave a mark, those that fill us with joy and those that tell us their stories although they repeat them again and again, I decided that everything is a gain according to my attitude facing situations and therefore it will never be too late to open my heart to a new friendship. I speak about female friends although I have many male friends too, and I also dedicate time to them and most of them are my counselors, to say so. With my female friends I've got gender empathy; who better than a woman to understand that you're tired of walking in heels, who better than a woman to understand that, sometimes, because of personal presentation, it's time to make sacrifices.

I have always dedicated myself to the business, and image is super important in it. It gets so competitive and hard.

You must wear high heels, and there are days that go by too quickly so when we realize, it's already night, and my feet suffer because high heels are more uncomfortable than they seems to be.

In this era where everything is technological, we chat online for anything: to expedite, for organization lack, or whatever it's called, but we are always depending on the phone; and even with technology available for our service there is nothing more complex than meet up with a group of friends, however small, even with just three of them is difficult to reach an agreement; so I decided that if I want to see someone I must call. It was difficult to get together for months, but we do; those reunions are magical, extraordinary for me, what moves me to be better every day, since these people are my mirrors where I see everything I love, and also what I need to improve.

I live in that constant learning and evolution, which comes to be the best of my life, I transmit what I feel to everyone I can, that energy that characterizes me and that love that overflows from every one of my skin pores.

No matter if we sit down to laugh at trivialities or if we talk about transcendental issues, the important thing is that when we hang out I feel that the whole world smiles and our souls dance and dance in a harmonic harmony, full of splendor and self-confidence. We talk about stories: good, bad and ordinary ones, but stories after all. We enjoy each thought, that's beautiful and wonderful, there comes the magic and it's incredible, but the women who do this daily, us, who share with friends, we vibrate in the tune of love full of confidence and eager to eat the world; who said fear! That's why I have friends!

My conviction is that nothing is right or wrong in life, when we judge or criticize we already give value to the material, to the ego and that leads us to negative things, without good there is no evil and without evil there is no good, (quotation that I love), in this way I have achieved more harmony in my environment.

Without light there is no darkness and without darkness there cannot be light, that is why at the moment when we stop being critical and we stop judging our surroundings, we begin to vibrate in the tune of love, and we go taking the difficult way of flowing, everything at its time; and each soul has its moment, to reach its evolutionary goal on this plane.

It's beautiful when we wake up to life and decide to see the world from another point of view, but without wanting to force anyone to do the same. That is the most wonderful thing, because those beings that help us in the process come to our lives. Everything arrives at the perfect moment, at the indicated one. And it's up to you, when you feel prepared, neither before, nor after, at the right time.

A MARK THEN AND NOW

It was a rainy day, a gray one, which most of the humanity do not love, I get up, I prepare coffee, and involve myself into the housewife role, it's Sunday and it's time to do housework, attend to the family, everything... tidy up, and cooking, cleaning, I receive an important message and I must go to take my son, the apple of my eye, with his father, it wasn't planned but it was necessary, we met the three of us and we talk about the child behavior, and we make it clear that any past situation it was arranged in peace and harmony for our family. When we breathe and feel the relief that everything is clear, that day as hand of fate I suffered a huge accident. On my way home, I was driving over a bridge when a tire of my car explodes and I lose control. It was raining, everything happened in no time. Suddenly it rains harder, and an inexplicable force took me over and managed to get me unharmed from so horrible accident.

As you can imagine the car was destroyed. My relatives who know me and know I drive fast, they can't understand how I'm alive; I didn't drive as usual that day, if I would, I wouldn't be writing these lines.

What I felt in those impact seconds, in that extreme situation, is only understood by those who have gone through something similar.

I didn't felt anguish, or despair, contrary to what I thought at some point watching news, at that moment I felt a peace that I had never experienced, and if it was necessary to have faced the beyond, just to feel that peace, I thank heaven and the universe.

When they help me out of the car since the door got stuck by the impact, I saw people from another level; it seems that I wasn't in my body. I didn't listen to them but I knew what they were saying and I saw them in slow motion although my logic understood that they acted with anguish and rush.

All this happened in seconds, although it seemed eternal; at some point I thought I had really died, but when I started to feel my body again and control it, at that moment I realized that I was alive, and also unharmed. I took control of the situation with the calm of someone who just woke up from a very deep sleep, I know that the words fail to explain everything I felt, but I'm doing my best, so that you can imagine what happened. Hours passed while the crane arrived and I explained what happened a hundred times or more, I talked to my son and told him how much I love him at the same time I thanked the universe because he was safe and sound with his father at that time.

To that place friends started to arrive, neighbors, and much community collaboration. Those who saw the accident agree that the tire explodes on the slope of the bridge's junction in a curve, and they don't know how to explain such a small woman achieve to control the situation, I don't know either.

Hours later, we got to have lunch with my partner and his children, they still reflected concern on their faces, and I just broke into tears. I wanted to talk to my mother, but knowing her I avoid telling her because she would have gotten sick.

That afternoon passed quickly, and at night after preparing dinner for everyone, I breathed and plunged into the deepest of dreams, the next morning I spoke to my son again, I blessed him, and attended to the boys. I organized everything at home and prepared to send a message to my closest contacts, everyone had the same reaction, and that's when one values the healing power of true friends. Each one gave what they had in his heart, what I received was about encouragement, comfort, and even nervous laughter just thinking that I had been saved once more from leaving this earth. That day I felt more love than usual and my loved ones know how I am, oversweet, but that day was the total overflow of feelings, and I decided to show them without looking at whom, or expecting absolutely nothing in return.

In life we go through, therefore, uncomfortable situations, some strong, misunderstood without the right to be clarified thanks to the ego, and that's the true. That's the reason why friends arrive and leave, the ones always remain, those who despite the distance, we know they are and will be there at the right time. All are loved as long as they know how to receive, those who don't accept that love, for any reason, know that as they shared a bit, they took a place in each heart, so we should, before supposing or assuming, to try the crazy "ask method"!

I understood that judgments and criticism are typical of the ego and the ego is the main manager of all wars, I understand that we all vibrate in different tunings, and many people come to our lives as mirrors of what we should improve in ourselves, those so-called teachers, with whom we have differences, those are the ones we should thank the most.

MAGICAL EXPERIENCE AND NATURAL CONNECTION WITH MOTHER EARTH

That moment when I decided to take the pictures for the cover of this book, and I think to do something as natural as myself, without filters, without touch-ups, without makeup, as a friend would say "without production".

I imagine the cover, with the most natural of me captured by photography, and I launch into the experience of being a model for an afternoon, what an experience!! Be a model is not easy; and I began to think how it would be with tons of makeup or reflectors used in most photographic studios... I'd die!

It isn't easy to transmit what you want to the lens, I hired as a photographer a great friend who is also a writer, sensitive, an artist; I knew she would capture what I thought of transmitting.

It's very difficult to pose for a camera, it was me all the time, but posing is an art, my respect and admiration for that artistic area professionals.

I leapt myself to three thousand photos or more, with heroine's courage, and there I was, without clothes!

With my favorite panties when I get tan, and nipple shields to cover my bust.

I faced the imposing of the sea, thanking life for so much... I enjoyed every moment of that session that much that I finished exhausted; I put my heart in each photo, and that was what I wanted to transmit. When I immersed my half-naked body into our Caribbean sea's water , and I feel like the sea comes into me, it's a sexy and very pleasant sensation, and I think that everyone at some point in adult life should experience that feeling so natural, without so much paradigm, for a instant free of prejudices, and get the risk with the joy of a child, that inner child we all have, who we leave in our psyche's oblivion; feel the joy of being alive, of breathing, to feel the sand on our bare feet, the water in every inch of our skin. That hasn't got comparison, and it is as simple as a decision, it's all that is needed, in order to feel all that magic, decide we are able to enjoy the simple things of life.

AN ACT BEHIND ANOTHER ACT

The day I decided to write, I didn't do it for another reason than getting to help people who agreed to receive help, because I understood that only those who want and accept to be helped really receive what they are looking for.

It was a long process and then having faced so many strong situations in my life, I had a revelation about my mission, and that was to provide everything that at some point I wished to receive when I was going through the worst. But then I understood that I wasn't prepared.

When we are willing to receive what we ask is like magic, everything is transformed, the universe really conspires to make everything happen, and we can distract a little from the goal but after the decision is made, one way or another, sooner or later, we will arrive.

When a dream is fulfilled, when a challenge materializes, we realize that, actually, that's not the end but the beginning of another, or other challenges and goals, it's life, life flows, and it's constantly in movement.

The secret is to go in constant harmony with its vibration, to keep up with the rhythm of the dance to make it clear.

I dedicate myself to advice companies and represent them, to achieve brand positioning, it isn't an easy task, and I'm so competitive.

I know many people every day, of those many have requested for support, and I have been doing it with pleasure, I give talks, at institutions, about ego, self-esteem and resilience; self-esteem for company's management and the ego as a destroyer of dreams, among others, because from my experience self-esteem was my savior on several occasions. Paradoxically these two terms are antagonistic and confused every day.

I have mental health professionals support who they have been a guide for several years, when I decided to face the world and help people, ordinary people who wasn't thinking to go to therapy, but they would like to talk with someone who has suffered something they are facing, and a friend to listen to them and be willing to clarify part of the situation from their perspective.

Talking to so many people isn't easy, it's a big challenge, but the satisfaction of reaching those who are willing to receive my point of view, I feel that I am putting my grain of sand in this world, so that we are more tolerant, and we can harmonize in our environment.

VIBRATING IN THE TUNE OF LOVE

Morning's dawn, a new day full of all the good my being reflects, I breathe and I feel like everybody cell wakes up at this dawn.

It's a reflective day, I go for coffee, but first I go through my son's room who is still sleeping, I look at the tenderness of him in his rest, and I can exhale only love, I kiss him, and I go out carefully to don't wake him up: I prepare my coffee, and I feel the smell awaken my senses even more, I face the computer at my home's terrace where I contemplate the calmed sea.

It's a day of reflections, I decided that from time to time I would take one day of the month and I would dedicate it mostly to think and mark a before and an after to continue evolving, it's something like a business cycle report but in a personal way, I understood that each person is in his or her evolutionary process and even if we try to move them forward with all the love, it would be like taking the fish out of water. I understand not always a friend is looking for you to fix the chaotic situation he or she is going through, it's more about giving some advice or opinion on how to get out of it, sometimes they just need to be listened. I understood those people who come into our life when everything gets complicated are teachers, and we can learn as much as our heart is open and be willing to do. I understood, by the way, that what we don't like about another person is precisely what we should improve in ourselves, and I'm not talking about physical appearance.

In this cycle I understood many things, and not always having understood means that knowledge is assimilated, we can repeat the lesson as many times as necessary until we really assimilate it, for this reason I think we never stop learning, in a single life, when we leave a part of us behind, we realize how important it's to keep the rest, and I decided to face myself, all I have inside me, to give value to the truly important and I understood that there're just a few: we really need to be in peace, harmony, and vibrate in the tune of love.

Material things are about the physical things, since we inhabit a body that by the mere fact of being materialized is already perfect, no matter the form, or how symmetrical it is, they teach us to venerate it and care for it since it's the soul habitat.

There are thousands of cultures and points of view, and they're respectable, all of them. I think feeling good and being healthy, it's most of the task, the rest will be achieved.

With time I realized that I don't need much, I can live perfectly with a little, and I got into the story of minimalism, this is something very personal, in a complex world of much materialism, it is not easy, but I learned to live with little, If I'm honest, the most complicated thing for me was to stay with just the necessary books, which I really love, those who are going to be reread, because I have read them several times, and that reduced my collection from more than five hundred books to a few tens, I put myself into the task to look for those books that were my treasures once, take them one by one and enjoying what touched me when I read each one of them, and I went packing in boxes, which went to public libraries, to my friend's, and even bookstores for buying and selling second hand books.

At first it was very difficult, but after taking out the first box, the rest was much easier. If a friend of mine, who likes reading as much as I do, (his house is upholstered with books) knows what I have done, he probably would be speechless for a while. As he knows how am I, I suppose he would be surprised with the magnitude of my decision, but he would know as well that these books will be read several times and they will share those emotions I felt to others and that's the reward for me. Having taken them out of my life, of my space, I did the same exercise with all my material stuff, and I began to investigate the subject, there are many people in the world who live with less material things, and I want to clarify that this topic is very personal. It doesn't mean that this is right or wrong, it's each one decision and must be respected, about this respect thing, I mean that if we have a family member or a friend who thinks differently, you may accept them without trying to change their opinion.

I think relationships must be based on respect, nobody owes us anything and we don't owe anyone more than the respect of letting be.

The paradigms of good and evil are complex, that's why societies are complex, and that's another issue, but if each one is dedicated to their self to their evolution, seeking their own balance, without trying to change anyone, the world would be different, personally, I have all colors, thoughts and styles friends, and I offer what I am to all of them: authentic, and with an open mind; it must be why each one is how they are, and we allow ourselves to be, they don't need to change and that must also be managed from the energy of love, it's the only way to move forward with any situation.

This of minimalism, I'm so happy that I wanted to write a chapter dedicated to tell you how it changed my life. Material things have come and gone in my life; I've lost everything, three times so far, and I have realized that what is really necessary is breathing, be alive and aware.

The first time was at my early age when I decided to live alone, and I left my grandparents' with whom I lived the first years of my life. At that time I had nothing, or so at least I hadn't paid it, I left home with a suitcase of clothes and another one of shoes; from that moment I realized that isn't necessary own so many things. Then little by little I was accumulating again, and so it happened twice more, but the time has come to raise awareness, and more with an environmental engineer brother who does nothing but talk about this subject, so this touched me and I decided to consume less.

At the moment I'm on a project with a friend, about precisely the issue of start using what we don't use, or giving it to a new owner. That project is brewing with great desire and we hope that soon it will be able to materialize.

I took many of my things, clothes, shoes, bags, accessories, etc… and I put myself into taking out what I didn't love , what I didn't use for long time, and I stay with what produces me joy and happiness, I haven't ever said that this task would be easy, it's also a hard work, because I had a lot of stuff and it took me months to do it.

When I was ready I took a big part of this and I donate it, I gave it away and I even sold what I could, and all that money was invested to make this book printed.

So as you can tell, love moves everything.

It was a process and I think I still have a lot to do, a long way to go on this topic and accept the challenge of follow that science, at my own pace, as it should be, without rush, but with all the desire to move forward and continue beyond my own paradigms.

Now I spend less time choosing what I'm going to wear every day, I change clothes less times a day, therefore, I wash less clothes, and the most important, I have more time for what's really important, my spirituality, my son, my family, my home, my friends, and all the wonderful universe that I have created so far in this earth.

To enjoy each moment as if I were the only one, and that's how I really feel it. When I am writing I give myself so much into it, that I really feel that's the only thing that exists, I enjoy it, I live it, and I take the necessary advantage to create my own universe second by second.

THE ROADS AND LIFE

Each one's life is unique, likewise each person is unique. I had an early in the morning meeting, at my son's school which is three kilometers away from home. I decided to jogging my way back, and when I jog, I think about it, it's a moment alone with myself, away from everything, from the noise, from the mind, I can manage to stay in that state of internal meditation, that's why I enjoy to work out so much, I started my race over the asphalt road and every step I took was tiring. I'm used to jogging over the sand of the beach, and that's why when I change the scene it always generates a bit of resistance. The inclement sun demanded more, but it's three kilometers only; I thought immediately. Since my last record was 18 Km, I give myself encouragement to move on. I reached a stretch where I had to step on the sand again, and it was even worse, since the sand was very loose, but I had to get home soon, and I couldn't go by the seashore where I need less effort, and specifically at that moment I realized that this is life.

Like the roads, sometimes we are prepared to follow them and as complex as they are we tolerate them better, the problem lies when we don't expect it, we aren't prepared to face the different, or more complex paths, stressful situations or difficult solutions; then frustration comes.

In the worst moments the healthiest thing is to breathe, relax a little and if necessary stop. Each one goes at their own pace and by their own needs.

Sometimes roads are not easy, they are complex. There are normal paths where we can get bored; whenever we reach a goal, the next one comes, and it depends of the evolution level in which each person can be found. It's beautiful when this reality is accepted and we become viewers instead of judges in our environment and in our life of each one of the people who bumps into our path.

THE GIRL NOBODY WANTED

Usually my talks begin with a short account of what was my life and what is nowadays, my story, thanks to so many hard situations, I gave myself the oportunity to start this work, and the idea is to leave my bit in this world, and to positively touch the souls who are able to receive the help or support they lask for, because sometimes that support or help is not requested or longed to face a situation or event. There also is peolple truly willing to receive it, but this can only be discovered at the particular moment when what they are asking for, and what you said to confronting them are face to face.

I thank life for making me different, although I went a long way to understand and recognize myself.

I am the love's fruit of those passionate teenagers who idealize fairy tales.

My parents in the midst of their age's uncontrollable and typical emotions, decided to marry secretly even when they were teenagers. In the transition from child to adulthood, both in high school, depending economically on their families, they got married in Santo Domingo's church in Cartagena distilling love by each of thcir pores. I was already on the way, although nobody but them knew of my existence; before this, my mother faced the hard decision of having me or had an abortion. My father was her first and only one, and she was too young.

At the end of all this internal war to let me come to this world, against wind and tide, I was born on a rainy day in July.

At this point my parents had faced the reality and responsibility burdens that weren't able to face yet.

When idyll and fairy tale had ended, became a horror story. When my mother suffered the consequences of knowing that her prince charming was of flesh and blood regular man, trying to move on from teenager to adult, and she finds out his many girlfriends, lovers and friends, one by one, which destroyed an idyllic love illusion. My father was at an evolutionary level far away from hers, that's why the relationship didn't work.

My mother with a withered heart and a newborn girl lived in pain, and I don't blame her for the difficult decision of leaving me with my maternal grandparents, since at her age and in her situation any of us would have done the same.

So I grew up with my maternal grandparents. My grandmother was misogynist, so from there I understood why my lack of femininity, and my grandfather's military regime, neither of them capable to give love, pampering, tenderness, or anything like that to give the emotional support that psychologists and mental health specialists proclaim today.

I grew up practically in a dictatorship, where I had no right to argue or comment anything, however they gave me economical support, it must be why I value more non-material things, and the material ones for me will always be secondary.

I stand out almost all my life at the academic part, and I was always the different girl, with extreme thinness, not because I didn't eat, my physical build was always like that, and I suffered bullying from my classmates, because of my hyper laxity, I always caused the circus clown effect, that's why I don't like circuses and much less clowns, I avoid as much as possible visit these places.

At the young age of fifteen I finished my high school and I started the university in the career that my father (grandfather) had chosen for me, business management, and against my will I left to study.

I did very well in that first semester but I decided at any price to go to what I really wanted, and it was surgical instrumentation, because I sign up and sneak in, with a lot of effort, secretly from my grandfather, with the courage of a national soldier, knowing that I could die trying, I always dreaded him more than I respected him, although he was a little, but only a little, more loving (if it can be called like that), that my grandmother. My grandmother could never smile, she always looked angry; they always made it clear that I was with them, not because they wanted to, but because they had no choice.

After second semester of my beloved career, my grandfather dies, and my world broke down, my grandmother never showed affection, and I felt as she hated me, so without much thought I went to live alone, at the young age of seventeen after a great fight with my uncle (my mother's twin brother, and also my grandmother's favorite), who with great pain for my grandfather' death, arrived and discharged all that anger and helplessness exposing his primitive brain to me.

Nobody cared what could happen to me, and I think that deep inside, my grandmother was so sure of the education and values she had taught to me that she didn't even flinch when she saw me leave.

A few years later of much effort, sacrifice, to finish my career and maintained myself, I graduated as a surgical instrumenter who was my greatest desire at those times, I went to my degree ceremony alone, and I ran to mourn to a room in the city center where I lived at that time, I don't remember much, I just know that I cried until my tears dried and I fell asleep, since what I desired the most in life and what I should be proud of, was something I never celebrated.

I met my father at business management's first semester and I confronted him, it was another reason to follow my dream and leave behind the career my grandfather had chosen.

I was around fifteen and it was very hard for me to find out his story version, but I decided to meet him and thanks to that decision today I have the most beautiful family in the world.

I met my brothers and his wife, with whom he lived much of his life (so she's my brothers' mother) and today I consider her as another mother, I love her all with all my heart.

A while ago I arranged a date to sit my father and my mother at the same table after twenty-five years without talking, so they finally put everything clear and they understood it was necessary to forgive and keep going.

My mother also has a family and from that union I have two brothers more, handsome, beautiful in every single way. I saw them born and I was with them many times, but I understood that it's not necessary to spend a lifetime with someone you love with all your heart.

I understood that you see your life as you are fundamentally. Life of each one is a reflection of what it's in their heart.

I saw each one of these situations as cruel and hard as they seem, from the love I am, that's why, in addition to accepting them all as they are, and respecting their different points of view and behaviors, I love them, convinced that we aren't anyone's judges, and we can live in peace and harmony while we are capable to leave the ego, and all its negative charge, what is commonly called make the suitcase lighter.

-THE END-

This book was completed in September 2019.

www.ingramcontent.com/pod-product-compliance
Lightning Source LLC
Chambersburg PA
CBHW081254130726
47998CB00010B/2791